TAPESTRIES OF A KINGDOM

Michele Gould

LYNMOORE
HOUSE

Copyright © 2023 by Michele Gould

All rights reserved. This book or any portion thereof may not be reproduced or used in any manner whatsoever without the express written permission of the publisher except for the use of brief quotations in a book review.

Printed in the United States of America

First Edition, First Printing 2023
Published by Lynmoore House
For information, email Contact@Lynmoorehouse.com

Hardback ISBN 979-8-9889684-0-5

Paperback ISBN 979-8-9889684-1-2

This is a work of fiction. Names, characters, places, and incidents are either the product of the author's imagination or are used fictitiously. Any resemblance to actual persons, living or dead, events, or locales is entirely coincidental.

To everyone who read something I sent them,
then gave me a reason to keep writing.

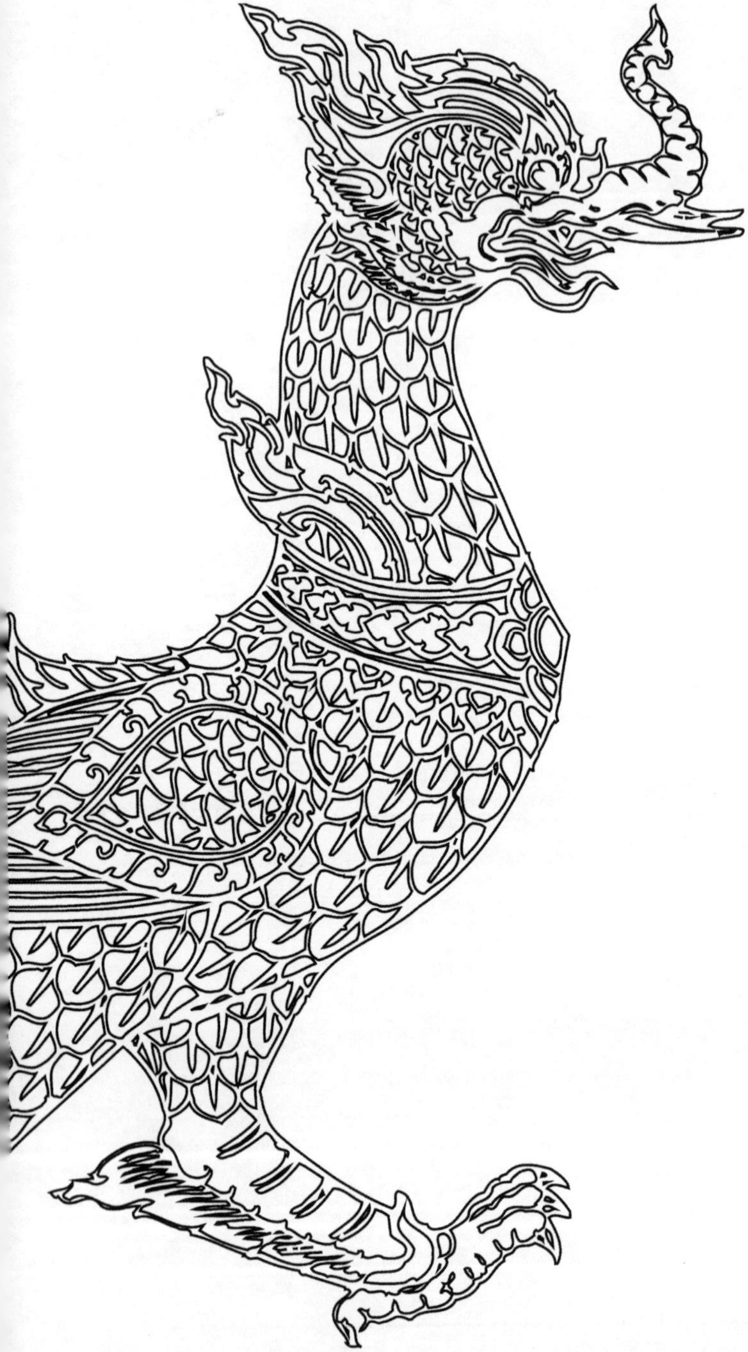

✻ ✻ 1 ✻ ✻

The tide decides what's left behind.
Break, bend.
Rage, end.
The tide decides, the tide decides.

Reader, did you know that we live in a closed system?

All the water that there ever was is all that there ever will be. The same water that fills the seas is the same that hails from the sky, and the same will fall into the rivers to meet itself again in the ocean. I like to believe that every drop of rain that's fallen on my cheek could have—at some point—also touched hers. If you could read the water like a book, how would the pages be numbered? Could the words bend the way that waves do? How do you trace the mind's wandering from spring to brook to river mouth? I suppose that's why they call it a stream.

All that is written grants us a beginning and an end; memories are not so forgiving. When I try to cup it all in the palms of my hands, to be still and let the ripples rest, all I seem to learn is what once was and what will change. A small mercy; with every scoop, her eyes are the same, as is her laugh. I let it all pour out and ladle another and another.

I rest on this bank when it's all too much. When the tide has battered and bruised my bones, and I am shaking from the spray. But knowing her was never about the shallows. Knowing her was looking out to the sea in the face of a growing storm and welcoming the rain. I can take you with me to the day that it all changed, but I will spoil it for you now; it all ends in flames.

* * *

In the tropical lands of Isira, you will find a kingdom starved of water. Tabashi, once known for its sapphire rivers and the long flowing channels in the fields, with oxen ploughing the rich dark earth from which our greatest resource grew: rice, bountiful bundles of it, golden stalks in rolling fields, enough to cover the entire stretch of land from the city to its shores. Can you just imagine it? The warm gilded hue of the sunset over a tawny sea. In my dreams, I find myself in those lands, circling like the herons over a field of rice, chasing after the koi fish swimming in the channels, their spotted orange and white-silver backs shimmering under the ripples of the water striders.

But the earth changed a few hundred years ago. We were told stories of the Great War that took place and the devastation that lay in its wake, of the lands we lost to the fire, of the drought that outlasted the people who could recount the tales. After centuries, Tabashi survivors were as thirsty as the rivers were dry.

Awake—and feeling very bold—I raced across them. Empty channels between the rice fields, my best friend at my side. Barefoot and brave-faced, we skipped over the broken earth the colour of crumpled tapa left out to bake—dirt crumbling under our heels. A new sun was rising and, even in the quiet early morning, beat its unforgiving heat down onto the parched land. It was the dry season in Tabashi, but I doubted either of us could recall a time when the seasons had changed.

We were trying to outrun the anger of a great and gentle giant: the ox, the guardian of the farms we trespassed on. Its grey stony humps rolled down the hills towards us, but it would never catch up; it was an old and retired beast, haggard from the years of toil, with nothing to reward its loyal service. Sweet when you offered it the husk of your discarded taro, less so when you teased it through the fence. It had gotten used to the greasy, prodding hands of kids with nothing else to do, and I imagined it could hear us coming from a village away. Could the ox enjoy chasing us as much as we enjoyed running from it? If only we knew how to listen for its laughter.

"Race you to the top!" she called to me, a swift wind flying past her, whipping through her plaid sarong that she'd hiked up and tucked into her waistband. She was many paces ahead and had leapt to climb the legs of a tall and rickety hut, perched on slim bamboo stilts and still standing, solitary in the empty field of an unsown land. It took me heaving all the air that was left in my lungs to catch up with her—and even then, only as quickly as my own little legs allowed. I raced to tell her how annoying she was, how she'd somehow cheated in the game we'd made up the rules for and quickly forgotten.

"They built them so tall!" I called out, hearing the words lost to the wind between us. One foot on top of the other, steadily climbing the wobbly frame. But then she replied.

"Can you believe that water once rose up this high?" and her voice was much closer to me than I expected. I looked up to see that she had stopped to wait for me on the top rung. I met her eyes there as well, dark like the skies above the sea in a storm and her hair like the clouds that filled it. "Come on, you gotta see this," she said. I reached out and grasped her outstretched hand, warm in mine, strong fingers curling around my sweaty palm. Up on the landing, I felt the weight of my body crinkle the soft bed of thinly handwoven straw beneath us. Flexible individual strands that when weaved together held fast. We looked out from the gaps in the scaffolding that held up the loosely thatched roof as it rattled above us, a gentle beating drum singing the songs of the wind over this land, calling to the rain as its people did. The lyrics of the song: we miss you.

We could see the entire field from that vantage point and caught sight of the herons that circled above, blackened gliding bodies in the shadows of the sun. I thought of myself sailing on the wind as one of them, trying to see the world from out of their high and hungry gaze.

"They're looking for the water too," I mused under my breath.

Looking out at the clear blue sky and the paper plateau below it, we noticed how the barren fields stretched all the way up until they reached the Jungle. The blurred edges of deep green trees blanketing the horizon; the climbing shadows in your dreams that you try to run away from lest it should reach out a thorny vine and catch you with it, dragging you back in.

I felt a sudden blunt stab in my ribs and looked around to her brandishing a cheesy grin and a pointed finger, demanding my attention. She led me to a hidden corner of the hut and threw off a jute tarp, revealing a stockpile of dried fish and mango fruit. A scent wafted up to meet us, salty and sweet. Thin and wide, the fish had a glistening sheen, like it was still wet from the water it had come out of. It smelled of the sea—and of smoke and ash. The mangos, wrinkled and translucent at the edges, were soft and grainy to the touch. It was then that we heard the guardian ox bellow from across the field below, having given up its chase, and the hut shivered in response. Our bellies grumbled, and we turned to face each other with knowing looks—forever bound by the mischief they promised. The sounds of our laughter, of ravenous children, faded into the morning sun—fading into the afternoon.

Despite my protests, time moved on from this place, as it always does.

* * *

"No sticky rice! For three days!"

"But—"

"But nothing! You kids have no respect," our teacher bellowed. We sat cross-legged in front of her, out the front of the Eyrell—our school—with prying eyes mounted on the nosy heads of the other kids peeking out at us through the open doorway. Our heads hung low, but our bellies were bloated and gloating.

"Those rations were for working farmers—not greedy children!" our teacher snapped at us, a grumpy-looking farmer beside her. His face had an uncanny resemblance to the oxen that guarded his fields. My friend snorted—a hideous sound—and I had to swallow a laugh I nearly choked on. Our teacher responded by smacking my friend across the head with a straw broom, so we both burst into a fit of giggles.

"Yo-d be'r watch it ne'time! Yo-ids dot'n no ew yer mes'n wit!" hollered the farmer, his words ringing out to fill the halls of the Eyrell. We all had to pause our riled cackling just to listen. His voice was so heavy with the drawl of country twang; we'd never heard an accent so thick before. Like a spark to kindling, our laughter roared, catching the flames of the snickering children ahead until we all became a field ablaze. Another whack. But our teacher soon abandoned any attempts to control us with the broom; we were too far burned for that kind of discipline to take hold. Sadly, she never budged on withholding that sweet sticky rice, steamed in a bamboo basket with the most delicate hint of jasmine.

Sticky rice was our currency at the Eyrell. Our teachers preferred it over plain rice as the leftovers could be kept and re-steamed and nothing would ever go to waste. But we rarely had enough to go around in the first place. Our bellies—as our days—were filled with shrieks and hysterics, followed by the unmistakable thwack of a splitting straw broom. Thin chickens scratched at our feet as we danced to avoid them, and bony stray dogs barked in the fray. We were wild because we were hungry. So we played, laughed, and caused all manner of mayhem. In those days in the Eyrell, in that tiny corner of Tabashi—the only kingdom without water in all of Isira—we chose unbridled joy.

Reader, as for that ending, I will set it alight when I'm ready. Memories are not so forgiving.

✷✷ 2 ✷✷

The sun beat down on the crowded coast as gentle waves curled in from the tide. I could smell the tang of freshly caught fish and the sweet coconuts brought to trade for them. The great blue expanse called, and as I found my way to the top of the dirt path, I finally caught sight of it in the distance. The real thing was much greater than any painting could conjure. It was something that beckoned to be felt, for how do you paint the breath in your chest that never deflates?

This was the moment I'd been waiting for: I would cross the borders and change my name one last time. I'd erase the past and so bring myself into a new future, one that I got to decide. I stood there in silence, watching the waves that lapped at the sandy shore and kicked up at the flat-bottomed sampans waiting in the bay, water-bound vessels that could take me far from this place with all the memories that lingered here, refusing to let me rest.

"Feast your eyes on these ancient artefacts!" a shirtless merchant hollered from beside me, sitting cross-legged on a mat, surrounded by his collection of curiosities and trinkets. I approached his stall and began to peruse the items on display out of politeness; I could not afford to purchase anything today that wasn't par for the course; it was hard to find a job that would take you without a proper name or any papers from your past. When the job came up about the ship to Petakai, I took it without question because it didn't ask any of me.

Amidst the merchant's seashells and handmade jewellery, I spotted a small golden necklace that seemed out of place for this seaside market. With a wry smile, the merchant lifted the artefact from its resting place and held it up for me to inspect. "You have a good eye. This one's very special; it's magical. It will protect you from all manners of beasts."

"Magical?" I asked, doubtful, admiring the intricate designs etched into its surface. The carvings of the face of a woman, with fierce and terrible stormy eyes and hair like the clouds that—

"All the way from Petakai," he replied, his gaze to the seas. I followed it, trying to find the distant kingdom he spoke of. The one I was headed to if the job I'd taken could be trusted. The kingdom of Petakai, another kingdom in Isira, was a straight path across the seas from Tabashi, a place I'd only read about in the history books donated to the Eyrell from the neighbouring villages. A school where you were lucky if you could find a quiet corner away from the barking of strays and the delighted screams of children. Somewhere you could actually hear yourself think, and only to do a thing not many other children thought was worth their time: reading. But I only loved it because it fueled the thing we all did: dream.

"Do you want the necklace? It can be yours for a bargain," he added with a cocky grin. "It belonged to Moultisjka the Terrible."

So that's why the image seemed familiar, because it had been burned into my head from all the old tapestries of the Great War, epic tales that were passed down from wise elders to tired teachers to their listless students. How the Greats and the Terribles had fallen, now finding themselves bargained for as cheap trinkets in crowded marketplaces. I rolled my eyes at his theatrics; I wasn't about to be swindled out of the few coins I had for his shiny but decidedly un-magical necklace. He could have fooled me with magic, but he lost me at Moultisjka, and names are precious things; they should be left alone lest their spirits come back to claim them, angered at their calling.

"Well, I wouldn't want her to catch me wearing it then," I replied, and he grumbled in frustration, returning the item to its place. I wouldn't show him the true fear that lingered beneath my dismissal. It was clear that he was not Tabashi-born; he'd been saved from a childhood of the kinds of stories that stay with you long past your youth. Moultisjka the Terrible would surpass them all.

Looking up from the vendor, I spotted, at the edge of the docks, an eviction notice posted on the door of a rundown shack: *By order of the Council, on behalf of the King;* then, scrawled in red ink and by a feverish hand across it, another bit of text. Translated, it wrote: *Not by blood.*

Reader, it's important to discuss translations. At the time you are reading this, this language is ancient to you. You should know that it once connected all of us throughout these lands, and after passing down its meaning through the miscommunication of time, this sentence can come to reveal two things: that is, "not by blood," as in a cursed accusation thrown at those who sit to rule in false pretence at the palace—the Council—and at the royal guards they paid to protect them. But also "not my blood," as in by all accounts of the Great War and the blood spilled on this soil in its wake, and the countless generations that labour and toil to bring about another harvest without the gift of rain, there is a right to refuse this ruler—by the power invested in the sacrifice of the people, looking to them for salvation. When it is spoken, in either iteration, know that it retains both meanings to the people bearing witness to the protest.

This language would remain the roots of all of our tongues—united by trade and a love of spices and delicate silks. Tabashi had welcomed people from so many different parts, its collective languages blending and shifting like the tide that brought them here in the first place. I couldn't tell you the tongue that was meant for me, my mother missing in the channels by which language is first taught. What I was, was the confluence of Tabashi's many rivers; I learned the script of merchants as I traded their stock, the longhand of nobility as I translated their letters, and the tones of the farmhands calling out across a dusty field competing with the crickets—their written language coming second to the nature of sharing stories through song. Their dialect would never end up in the history books. It is a tongue that cannot be severed from the people, or from their land, the same way that there is music without words; it can only be felt. Passed down through the generations as a lullaby from a forgotten time when the fields were flourishing, and the channels between them filled with a reflection of the sky.

The elders say that at night you can still hear their songs being sung by the breeze. They say that should you hear your own name whispered, then you should be careful. It's the sound of your ancestors calling. It's the sound of unconditional love—in the gift of a warning.

* * *

I made my way towards the docks where I would find the bigger ships. I had to push my way through bustling crowds that had been drawn to the colourful small vendors littering the coast—to the curious trinkets they sold. These marketplaces were so different from the ones further inland, boasting selections of dry rations for the journey across the sea and prayer beads beneath signs that warned of its dangers. Then, jumping out at me as if it were alive, a warning sign: the image of a giant snake beneath the ocean's waves, twin glowing eyes, and its mouth circled into a snarl.

"Beware the naga!" a merchant called out to me from behind a row of crooked teeth. "They say that any pitiful sailor unlucky enough to gaze into its open jaw will look up at a sky full of stars before he is swallowed into them."

Suddenly I heard a commotion up ahead. It was a danger more urgent than the warning of the seas. Curses were being thrown at the Council by a woman clothed in red, perched on a barrel and waving her arms at the crowd for their attention. She would be stopped soon—I was sure of that—by palace guards falling upon her like a blanket of rain over the distant jungle canopy. Even though there were only ever a few guards this far out from the city, the Council made sure there were always a pair of eyes to keep watch, to quell any disquiet that might arise in their well-kept kingdom. I kept to the shadows of the others, trying to weave my way through the noise unnoticed.

"Not by blood! Curse the Council's false reign," the woman jeered, and my mind flashed back to the scrawl of red ink on the eviction notice at the edge of the docks, "and curse the Exorci they hide behind!"

I heard a few responses from the crowd then, people who shouted in support of her protests. She could have been the culprit in question, having defaced public property, demanding public accountability. But she could also just be one of the many—finally calling power into question. The crowd's impassioned cries were soon drowned out by the low and loud drawl of a buffalo-horn sounding out across the harbour. I froze, terrified, as flames from my past filled my vision: the figure of an ox climbing up through the depths to grasp at a girl falling backward into its fiery rage and a hand reaching back out towards me, racing against the blaze.

"Holy water!" someone yelled beside me, making me jump, and the memory vanished into smoke, replaced with the whirling rush of other patrons scurrying about to get to their ships. "Tame Exorci fires with this!" they continued, desperately holding out the bottle to gain the attention of people passing by, "then cut them with blades to bleed them of their powers!"

Shi help us, I thought, disgust swirling across my face. It was one thing to hate the Exorci; it was another thing to hurt them. This was a common tactic in the kingdom: to throw empty threats at the thing they didn't understand. No one had any proof that these tactics worked, but fear could strike as violently as any blade. Exorci were people—children—who happened upon ancient magic, sought by the Council, and then thrown into service of their wars. Exorci did not choose to set the world on fire; curse the people who blamed them for that.

I felt a rush become like a tide behind my eyelids. Reader, I am not an Exorci, but I understood their plight. The words cut me down as if they'd meant them for me—when at once, a waterskin containing the supposedly blessed water burst open. Its contents spilled onto the sandy path.

"Shi have mercy!" the merchant screamed, confusion and terror spreading across their face. I adjusted my robes and weaved my way back into the ongoing surge of foot traffic, blending back into the mix and wincing at the display. I couldn't let myself get carried away like that again; I had to pull myself together until I was on the ship and safely bound for Petakai.

It was then that I realised that I was late—and my clammy hands quickly found the palm leaf ticket tucked into my waistband that permitted my passage across the seas. I would find the ship, then promptly sail out of there with the tide that carried it, thinking to myself, *A chance for a fresh start, a chance to disappear, a chance to move on.*

** 3 **

The shorebirds cawed above as I stepped onto the well-worn planks of the bustling harbour, surrounded by boats of all sizes, each with their own crew dressed in colourful sarongs and plaid-check fabric, surrounded by plenty of coconuts. Someone raced past me to catch a sampan that had kicked off from the long jetty, and my eyes followed their flight to a mother hugging her child. My attention lingered there for a moment too long—and as I tried to pull my eyes away, I nearly stumbled back in shock. Coming into focus at the end of the docks was a fully grown kunchuwarri. I flipped through the palm leaf manuscripts in my memory like I was re-reading them in the Eyrell.

The creature was an elephant with the body of a fish. Born in and loyal to the sea, its bluish-grey skin ended in fins that faded into translucent tips along its spine, the backs of its ears, and its two front legs. Its tired gaze, the colour of long-buried stones, observed the surrounding chaos—numbed to the commotion. Its large ears flapped gently, cooling itself in the heat of the day. The rear half of its body submerged, rough terrestrial skin transitioning seamlessly into the scales of an immense tail swishing about in the shallows. Said to be rare and shy creatures—avoiding contact with people unless absolutely necessary—we considered seeing one a sign of good fortune, a blessing from the sea. Paintings had taught me a kunchuwarri should be slightly larger than a full-grown jungle elephant, but this one appeared considerably gaunt; strapped into a harness of rope and leather and tethered to the shore, its broad trunk was being used to hoist large barrels onto the neighbouring ships.

The mahout that tamed it stood wearily beside it, his hands clutching a minacious long steel hook. I shuddered at the thought and, without being able to stop myself, started towards the creature, feeling the familiar rush of a storm gathering within. But just as the tide had built and threatened to break itself against my temple, I shut my eyes to tame them, thinking, *Not again*. I couldn't afford to draw any more attention. Not if I was to get out of there, finally, and for good.

I averted my gaze and spotted the biggest ship in the waters, the only one of its kind moored in the harbour and fitting the description on the job advertisement. It towered above the others—long and narrow, with richly hued wood and elegant curves. I'd only ever heard about the harbour from my time drifting between Tabashi's many villages, but even this ship looked far more majestic than any other that could have frequented these waters. We had dreamt for so long of adventures across the ocean, staring up at the night sky and using the stars to guide us across it. *We*, a painful sentiment; I let it curl and pass over me, attempting to fix my gaze on the present.

The sailors nearby had eyed me with suspicion. They were probably wondering what I was doing gawking at their expensive ship. Likely, the equally expensive kunchuwarri beside it. Around me sailors unloaded cargo, merchants haggled prices, and travellers disembarked—all from different walks of life. Gazing down at my drabs: plain and dirtied orange sompot chong kben—cotton I had wrapped around my legs—with a wrapped bandeau to match. I had a light satchel for my few belongings, and I saw myself looking as lost as a fish pulled from the ocean.

Approaching the sailors preparing the large vessel for departure, I held out my ticket to them, asking, "Is this the ship bound for Petakai?" My confidence was unnatural, and my attention flickered between the ship and the kunchuwarri as it hoisted another large barrel. It saw me watching it—and paused for half a breath before the mahout tensed his grip around his hook. The mahout shot me a look of warning, and I snapped back to the conversation at hand.

"This is the very one. Behold the *Bayanihan*," one of the crew replied, "one of the first-ever penjajaps—and the greatest sea-faring warship in all of Isira."

I'd never even heard of a penjajap, let alone the name *Bayanihan*, and what was all that talk of war?

"Warship?" I echoed cautiously. The others chuckled.

"Let her get her sea legs first, Captain, before you go scaring her off. We can't have another one bail," called out one of the sailors as he made his way below deck. *Another one?*

I turned back to the woman I'd been speaking to, realising then that he meant *she* was their captain. The lengths of her brown sompot had threads of yellow embroidery and were wrapped around her sea legs, and across her chest she wore only a sun-bleached cotton blouse and a harness for her waterskin. She was decades older than me, having clearly had her fair share of time under the sun, but the captain had appeared so unassuming that I had mistaken her for just another member of the crew. It was then I noticed the large and tired machete strapped to her waistband. That weapon commanded a wise presence that surpassed her disarming charm.

"Captain Tanhchana Wardhani, pleased to make your acquaintance . . ." she said as her words drifted to make space for my response, and I raised my chin to address it.

"Linh," I said confidently, as I had done many times before. She returned a curious expression, but she didn't enquire further about the name—or lack of a title.

"Are you here to keep our records in check?" she asked.

I held my ticket out towards her, and she quickly retrieved it. That's when I noticed my hands were trembling. Though I could wear a mask of confidence from the neck up, it seemed the rest of my body was bound to betray me.

"If you'll have me," I replied and tried for an innocent smile. The captain briefly scanned my ticket and handed it back to me in a flash.

"Well, you can start by counting these barrels," she ordered, tossing her head back to gesture at them, "and make sure none of them go missing."

I spotted a fresh stack of lontar and a sharp metal stick for carving it—left on a barrel, probably from the previous employee who had been "scared off." Heading over to the materials to get to work, I found another reason to give me pause; I'd seen better records scratched at the village markets for merchants counting stacks of rice—before they'd even learned to read and write. It made me wonder whether I really had found the right ship, the one meant for crossing the sea to trade valuable supplies with the ones to be found in Petakai. Why had it all been so easy? That I had happened upon the job and that I was one of the capable few who had shown up to take it. I noticed a glinting in the sunlight of all the other machetes strapped to the crew of the *Bayanihan*.

"Captain Wardhani," I called out quickly before she left, "sorry, but why would you have a warship if this cargo is intended for trade?"

"'Captain.' Just 'Captain.' Listen, the people on these lands may have ambitions for trade, but they built the penjajap for what's out there. No point carrying all those goods to leave them resting at the bottom of the ocean," she replied, testing me. I looked back at the kunchuwarri, and at the steel blades and menacing hooks that littered the harbour—now made obvious to me. The harsh heat of the afternoon sun deepened the stale stench of the damp. I could feel the sweat beginning to form as I stood there by the barrels.

"And the kunchuwarri?" I asked, a stone forming in my throat. *Too many questions.*

"These aren't our docks," the captain replied coolly. I thought I'd caught a wave of sadness in her answer, but then, "So tell me, are *you* our records keeper?"

I swallowed hard and reminded myself of why I was there, that if I wanted to keep myself safe, I'd better stop asking things that could get me into more trouble. Thinking, *A chance to disappear, a chance to move on.* Standing up taller to meet her gaze, I nodded and put metal to palm leaf. Looking around at the barrels and then back down at the records, I furrowed my brow, trying to make sense of the letters. The captain must have noticed as she addressed me one last time before moving on with her duties.

"Rice wine," she answered with a wink.

Someone had written these records in the script used by the village people. I recognised it instantly, but I was still just learning to use it myself—the design passed down from the ancestors who wrote their records using palm leaves as paper, noting down important information by carving it into the flat of the dried leaves. Being ridged material, they had to write with the curl of the grain to not tear it—and so the language came from the trees that shaded the people as they wrote as a reminder of where they were from and the land on which they belonged. Looking at the *Bayanihan*'s records, I read three barrels: ꢀ, six stacks: ꢁ, and made some new markings of my own.

That afternoon, I busied myself with my work—counting the *Bayanihan*'s stock before they loaded it into the cargo hold—as the rest of the crew continued with theirs. Accompanied by the sounds of creaking hulls, the lapping of waves, and shouts of orders. Every now and again I heard the unmistakable low grumble of the kunchuwarri as it shifted in its harness.

I could see sailors hauling textiles and ceramics onto sampans, or hoisting bags of spices onto ox-drawn wagons bound for the marketplaces. I wondered if those goods would make it inland as far as Kern. Merchants called out their wares, offering pungent durian and carved ivory for trade, while others were hawking freshly caught fish and crustaceans. Around me were the faces of pedestrians as they looked upon the *Bayanihan*, then out to sea. I heard them praying, whispering to Shi. What did they think was out there? I thought perhaps I was the only one who didn't know and had my own reasons not to ask—the only fool in the kingdom who would take a job with "no experience required." But I wasn't just a fool; I was a desperate fool, and this job had come at the right time and was my only option.

The planks beneath my feet were slick, and I had to watch my step as I weaved my way around the stock meant for the *Bayanihan*. There was, in fact, more on offer than just rice wine; I found bundles of golden stalk and tamarind, dried fish and mangoes, and freshly harvested coconuts tied with straw. What would they purchase with these goods? What trade awaited us at Petakai? Trade that was worth braving the perilous seas and whatever was lurking beneath them.

As I rounded the corner to a quieter part of the docks, I thought I saw a flash of red across an otherwise perfectly blue horizon. I whipped my head up from my study, only to be met with the view of an empty landing, save for the stacks of goods I'd already counted. The salty sea breeze picked up as if taunting me and carried with it the sour smells of the age-worn docks. I involuntarily scrunched my nose in response.

"Hello?" I asked the breeze, but got no reply. *No questions asked*, I reminded myself—and again busied my mind with my work. *A chance for a fresh start, a chance to disappear, a chance to move on.*

* * *

"So where did all the water go?" our teacher asked, my attention drifting back into the classroom where we all sat cross-legged, our bellies grumbling before dinner time. We were all silent. Our teacher called out to me. I sat up from where I was and felt the pause in my friend's hands from where she sat behind me to braid my hair.

"In ages long past—" I began and heard my friend have to hide her giggle in a cough. I swatted her with my hands and raised my chin. "A long time ago, Anamashta the Great came to this land to provide for its people. From her magic flowed all the water and the fish in the fields and the rice that grew tall in the harvest."

"Very good, it seems you have been paying attention," our teacher mused and turned back to the class at hand, "though I can't say the same for your friend."

I was jabbed in the ribs from behind; I couldn't help the yelp that erupted from me.

"Girls," our teacher warned, "you're only sitting together again because I finally allowed you to." After we silenced ourselves with a sharp intake of breath, our teacher continued. "It's only natural then, in the balance of things, that there should be another to oppose Anamashta and her way of life."

I felt the surge around the room of an eager breath.

"Moultisjka the Terrible and her way of fire."

I felt them all exhale as silence fell.

Of all of our teachers' stories and the lessons they repeated, we would always listen to the ones about the fire. There was nothing like the magic of bending circumstances to your will, especially for children whose circumstances have always been the kind you endure, not enjoy.

We were told that Moultisjka grew jealous of Anamashta's power, seeking only to destroy what she could not grow, consuming it in flame. I recalled the painting of a terrible black beast, a giant ox that stood upright on its two hind legs, eyes of flame, carrying off the soldiers who had tried to tame it. A creature cursed to guard the evil things that Moultisjka had made out of the charred remains of Anamashta's love. This was the cause of the Great War; a fight for the land, and thus what the land became; a barren place for burnt beings.

I looked behind me, and my friend and I quietly shared a look, pretending to shoot an invisible power out of our hands at each other—pretending to be burned by it. We didn't know about the Exorci yet, about the ways we should be terrified if they discovered us to possess the powers we so craved.

"Anamashta did the only thing she could do. For Tabashi, she sealed her and Moultisjka away, lost in time, in the deepest parts of the Jungle, never to return."

The Jungle.

Reader, I should tell you now that contrary to the terrifying stories the adults would tell us about it, there is a moment when the Jungle is quiet. Even cicadas have to sleep. It's right before dawn, before the caws to the morning's light. You first see mist. Then, from high in the treetops, you bear witness to the breaking of the sun—warm on the shore of the horizon. Light catches on the dew on the leaves; and like gulls to the sea, the Jungle has its wardens. They fly across canopies, surveying the land. Watching for a change. Calling to the sunrise. Birdsong wakes with you, and the smells of the damp are like nothing else: crisp, clean, and intoxicatingly alive.

This is the best time to catch its beauty if you are, like me, so easily afraid of the dark.

I am telling you this because the rest of my account will tell you of the dangers of the Jungle. Of the creatures they taught us humans to fear. Nagas, creatures of the sea with the bodies of snakes the size of rivers, and even the peaceful kunchuwarri—rising from the deep and roaring in battle with the army it summons to protect its own. Feral monkeys guarding the borders of the Jungle, for those who wander too close, trying to control it—led not by a sound mind but a trembling heart. But there is only danger in what we don't know, and, at the time of this writing, you could fill a book with what I didn't know.

"Rumour has it that Moultisjka still roams about in the Jungle," our teacher continued, all of us on the edge of our seats, "waiting for an unsuspecting child with the gift for magic to wander too close—" We all leaned in, eager for her to finish her story. "So that she may catch them all and eat their hearts!" she shrieked, smacking one kid on the head with her broom. We all jumped and screamed with frightened delight and ran out of the classroom in a frenzy. The roaring fun of children—unbridled and spent by the end of the day to welcome a wistful night full of fantastic dreams.

I ran with my friend into the playground, and she whipped up some sticks to challenge me to a duel. She was such a fighter and an excellent one at that. Tall, athletic. What skill she wielded with her weapons I matched with my words and whimsy. Sadly, poetry wasn't on the list of crops to grow or ways to cultivate them. If it ever upset me, the way things do when you're that age—like a hole in your chest that grows and grows and threatens to swallow you up should you let go of your legs—then she would be there, helping me to hold them.

Reader, you might wonder why I am not disclosing her name—this far into the tale and with your gathering trust. Well, as I have mentioned, names are powerful things. Perhaps the reason I never called hers was because I was afraid of what would answer. We don't get to know why these things happen. It's only after that we can make it all make sense. I've found the best way to tell this story is to start it at the end of ours, because this is how it happened to me too. Reader, know that our hearts are breaking in tandem—and let there be some solace in that.

Why was I tracing the rivers of my past? Following the currents to where they pooled around the girl and desperately plunging my head? Submerged until my body tore itself away, gasping for air? I think because I was about to leave them all behind, and the memory was worth what it took to hold. Perhaps because, even in pain, at least they could still be felt.

How I wonder what the world would be like if it honoured the quiet prayers of children.

✻ ✻ 4 ✻ ✻

"All aboard!" the captain called out, pulling me from the depths.

I watched as the faces around me darkened. If the paintings and warnings on the docks were anything to go by, then this crew, and the weapons they wielded, had their work cut out for them.

I let go of the sensations guarding my chest and breathed out a heavy sigh, quickly gathering all of my materials and making my way to the others. I counted and re-counted the stocks. If there were any mistakes, it was because I could no longer read the numbers, having spent so long staring at them. It was one of the few respites I had to tune out a busy world, reading or writing as the waves swirled and crashed like cyclones against the mountainside. In words and numbers, I could find my peace. It was a different sort of magic, one where you pour circumstance into perfect glass jars and arrange them on the shelf for display. Though it is my preferred medium, life is the subject—in all its magnificence. We can never truly equate the two—but the poets will try.

Tabashi proper was a barren wasteland, littered with slow- and low-growing shrubs in dusty fields with sun-bleached stalks of rice that towered over them. You could find richer soil in the Jungle, but it was a treacherous giant that surrounded the kingdom. Bordering villages committed some people to the dangerous task of venturing in to gather what water they could. But with the risk so high, it was often like trading a life for a life. This was what they left behind after the Great War: shrapnels of people and their scattered livelihoods, scraped together with the force of memories of a greater time. It's amazing how Greatness endures, despite the Terrible.

Tabashi's other border was a never-ending ocean. Water surrounded us, enough to cover the entire kingdom, but they drained us from it. The Council had promised to build aqueducts to feed the people and the land, but they never finished their construction—always with some reason to delay: trouble in the north, an attack from the Jungle, a war to prepare for.

I had spent all my years on those dry lands, trying to remain as anonymous as my birthright. Disappearing from town in the middle of the night when its people had asked too many questions about where I came from and why I was there. Fleeing like a coward when someone I could depend on had wanted to depend on me in return. It was too hard, Reader, to admit that I needed them too. It was the tangled threads of a truth I would spend all my next years unravelling.

I had closed off so much and done it so many times that one day I woke with a partner in a room she wished she'd raised her kid in. The kid in question had wandered too far in search of water for her hungry family. But by the time they'd realised she was gone, it was too late. No one in the village had dared to cross the deep green night to find her. I had shown up in time to help my partner grieve her loss, thinking that our shared pain was enough of a lifeline, but there is more to love and life than what has broken us.

It inevitably came time for me to leave. I thought I had no other choice. But it was too soon; it would always have been too soon. It's terrifying how much damage you can create, even when you're trying to not exist.

* * *

In the Eyrell courtyard, playing with sticks or planning our next escape into the surrounding fields—that was where you would find us. Watching as the farmers peeked out at us from under their wide-brimmed conical hats. They sometimes looked like straw-coloured lily pads floating in a grey pond. We would always wave to the oxen as their great stony humps pulled along a plough, surfacing the dirt found buried beneath the topsoil, darkened earth that had attempted to grow our crop the season prior. You could never say we didn't try. Distracted, my best friend caught my ankle with her stick.

"Got you!" She smirked, retreating to a poised stance, waving her stick like a machete.

"Ow! That hurt," I carried on, a cheeky grin betraying my cadence.

"Don't get distracted then," she replied and readied herself for another round. "You'll never be an Exorci at this rate."

The magical soldiers of Tabashi. Enlisted by the Council to help defend the kingdom against the monsters that crept in from the ocean or from the endless perilous pit of the Jungle. She and I would spend nights on the thatched roof staring up at the black sea, talking about how we would become Exorci together to get to travel all over Tabashi, and maybe even to the east, to Petakai. We hadn't yet learned to fear magic.

"Hold this for me," I told her, handing her my stick.

"What for?"

"I'm going to use magic," I teased.

"Aren't you afraid Moultisjka will eat your heart?" she jeered. But as I held out my hands and concentrated on the sticks, my face collected in on itself. Concern spread across hers.

"Hey, I don't—" she began, but I'd stopped hearing her.

When you don't know what a thing means, it never truly feels real. We knew we would one day leave the Eyrell. We knew we wanted to stay together. I'd never seen magic before, but as I concentrated, something clicked.

My mind swirled with dreams of what I wanted; I thought of a home, a title. I thought of her, and I thought of the sea. It was a distant echo—like a whisper carried by the wind. The air crackled, and I felt it. So tangibly, so vibrantly. It was as if a door had opened and there was nothing to stop me from stepping through.

But nothing happened. The silence was almost deafening until suddenly—my belly grumbled; we roared with laughter. She ran to me with her stick and fell on me. We wrestled on the ground, giggling and kicking up dust clouds of straw until the dogs started barking.

I would grow to miss those days the most. The uneventful ones, when all we had was an empty belly and a head full of stories. When we would not know fear—or lack. I realised much too late that something had clicked, a door had opened—there was just no water to rush in through it.

* * *

The crew of the *Bayanihan* assembled on the deck before their captain, her voice rising high above the chaos of the harbour, slicing through the noise like she wielded her machete to do so. Despite the confidence that her leadership inspired, I could sense their unease. They were familiar with their orders. They had likely made this journey countless times. But the thought of setting sail once more would still gather a dark cloud—one that I was regrettably missing. I had thought to stop one of them in their tracks to ask for some sort of reassurance—a clue of what was to come—but they were all too busy, and much too proud to falter.

It was then that the sound of the buffalo horn once more blanketed the bustling harbour, dampening the discord into a single call to which we all tuned in. The sound was a deep and primal cadence from the creature they had severed it from. I felt the sensations seep in; it was the feeling of like calling to like. I fought to resist its influence as I gingerly stepped onto the wooden deck myself. The wood groaned beneath my feet. I envisioned a thousand deaths, half expecting the boards to buckle and give way beneath my weight, to send me soaring through an endless collapse, my meek body at the mercy of the waves.

But as I took in the salty air once more, I felt only the gentle sway of the vessel beneath me—not becoming me. I realised the wooden planks were meeting my feet with solidity. It was strength that surpassed my own. The shipbuilders of the *Bayanihan* must have spared no expense in making it the greatest seafaring warship to cross the ocean. A penjajap, I reminded myself, and thanked them with a prayer.

Both feet planted, I let the thoughts pool in: *This is my first time on a boat. We were meant to do this together; we were meant to do a lot of things together.*

I had spent decades in the drought. I was born into a search for the water like the herons that circled above. It was almost too much to bear now—the ocean all around me. I have always been called to it, strangely soothed by the thought of sinking beneath the surface. It took everything within me to contain the surge. The sensations that I'd spent the long days trying to hide. The power that meant I had to disappear, that I could never stay where someone would eventually find out. There was a name for the tamers of fire—for the magic that flowed from them. I had forgotten the name for those who could contend with them. If I knew then what I know now, I'd have known that the reason I could handle all the water was because I'd already practised drowning it out.

As I made my way to the central area of the deck, the crew hurried about around me, each one of them preoccupied with their own arduous task. Ropes were being hoisted, sails unfurled, and within moments we pulled away from the jetty. I felt the gentle shift as they pulled the final tether to the shore. The wind caught the sails. I thought back to the remarks about having legs prepared for the sway; mine were not. As the *Bayanihan* gained speed, I had to take my legs, shaking, over to the other side of the deck to brace myself against the much sturdier balustrade. But there was nothing dispiriting about my first experience on the penjajap—on the contrary, I felt myself flying. Water lapping against the sides like a lullaby. Ahold of the bannister, I could lean into the movements, grateful for an uneventful departure.

Unsurprisingly, as soon as I had allowed myself to relax, commotion erupted in the harbour; the kunchuwarri bellowed, its massive shore-bound bulk shaking the ground as it yanked itself free from its moorings, cut ropes ricocheting off the surrounding barrels with such force as to whip the wind into hissing. The mahout that once tamed it cried out in desperation, struggling to regain control of the situation—but it was too late. The kunchuwarri roared again. As a last act of defiance, its trunk lashed out and grabbed the mahout, lifting him up and flinging him out towards the sea like the fisher discarding their unwanted catch. The mahout would likely survive the experience, but it was surely one he would never forget.

I couldn't help the smile that accompanied the kunchuwarri's swift departure from the harbour, perfectly underscored by the helpless cries of its defeated captors, watching as the gentle giant returned to the sea—going home. I heard a low chuckle from above me and turned my face upwards to see the captain's, her hands at the helm of the *Bayanihan*. She had a grin on her face as wide as my own.

"Was that your doing?" I called out to her over the roar of the waves, the chaos of the harbour fading with each passing tide.

"I don't know what you're talking about," she called back evenly, accompanied by a wink.

✲ ✲ 5 ✲ ✲

As we left the shore behind, the sea grew wilder and the *Bayanihan* began to rock and break against the tides with more force. Marked by the groan of the damp wood as it settled into the function of its design, the penjajap breathed life as real as those who boarded her. Thinking of the ship cutting through the waves like the well-placed aim of one of the many machetes carried by her crew—a blade cleaving a way through the water, just like those machetes—it was our job to respect her and care for her, to keep off the rust so that she may serve us well in our time of need.

My legs were already weary, but despite this, I found a giddy laughter escaping my lips every time the *Bayanihan* broke the waves—sending the ocean spray up to meet our faces on the deck. The crew, so used to the sensations, moved around me like a stream collecting down the spine of a leaf, and I tried my best to fall into step behind them.

There was nowhere to escape the dry sun back in Tabashi, no shade and no relief from the thirst. It was like holding your hands above a fire and hoping it would burn out before you did. I knew everyone suffered without water, but I could not explain the nature of my dehydration. It was a thirst that wasn't quenched by drinking, even in excess. I could find some relief in the shade of a dying tree and grew to wander closer and closer to the edges of the dangerous jungle as I got older. I wasn't able to resist my instincts—and it didn't help that we lived so close to its border.

But on the open seas, I could at least find solace from the drought; it had plagued my every waking moment. Being on the water was beyond anything I could have imagined. I thought my feet had not found their balance in the harbour because of a fear of the deep, but it was actually because I was trying to stand up against the never-ending sensation of falling. The ocean was so vast, and its depths infinite. How can I describe what it felt like to float above it all? Someone who has been thirsty their whole life? If I let my thoughts drift, even for a moment, the waves that found me would send me crashing into a torrent from which I feared I would never surface.

I spent that first day exploring all the nooks and crannies of the *Bayanihan*, all of its rigging and polished woodwork, detailing the penjajap with my keen eyes and tracking the movements of the crew to learn their routines. As I roamed, I approached one of them who seemed between tasks. She stopped as soon as she noticed me, so I met her quickly with my words. "Excuse me, sorry, but I'm so curious; what does the ship's name mean?"

"Penjajap is the build," she replied, looping a long piece of rope around her wrist and forearm. "It's the signature of the shipbuilders. *Bayanihan* is the name of all of us, for what it takes to sail her; it means community."

With her head held by the high tide of pride, she took off to catch a wayward rope flurrying in the breeze. I looked around to marvel at how the ship was so perfectly suited to its name. I was merely a visitor there on the runnings of a ship with its crew like family. The sound of the wind whistling through the ropes, the crashing sea beneath us, and the rustle of the sails above—I felt them all completely. The great expanse inspiring a feeling of freedom, I guessed, and of adventure, a feeling like running through an open field, laughing in the sun—her hands in mine.

Enough.

Wanting to distract myself from the thoughts that lingered, I decided I would check my records of the stock. I made my way below deck into one of the storage hulls. I had to brace myself against the walls as the *Bayanihan* rocked. In the chamber's dark, I could hear more clearly the creaks of the wood and the sound of the ocean breaking against it.

As I made my way through the barrels, I checked the inscription on one. From behind me, I heard a step I didn't place. I spun around just in time to catch a blade at my throat. Staring down the length of the machete, I beheld a masked stowaway covered in crimson. They had wrapped themselves from head to toe in the stained material with cotton rags and bandages that held up a chest piece of leather armour—a warrior in red.

"You saw me in the harbour," she accused, the warning in her voice gripping my throat harder than the threat of the blade. My mind raced against the waves that came crashing in around me.

"I didn't," I replied quickly. *Shi help me*, I thought. *Is this how I die?* Below deck and stumbling into dirty business I had never meant to be a part of.

"Good answer. How about now? What do you see?" she spoke again. In a moment not long enough to take in a breath, I took her in: the sweat on her brow, the intensity of her stance, the steadiness of her grip on the machete. Though she had covered most of her face in the material, in the little light that filtered in from above deck, I could almost make out a pair of dark storm clouds staring right back at me.

"Nothing," I said listlessly.

"You're getting it. Good," she recovered, withdrawing the machete to strap it back in place by her hip. Could she read my passivity? Surely there was no reason to bring about more suspicion on her part with my sudden disappearance from below deck.

"What do you want?" I asked.

"To do my business and disappear. So if some of these

barrels are missing from your records, you never saw them either," she finished coolly.

That was all she wanted? Some falsified records for her own gain? Could I risk death by her blade for some rice wine gone missing? *No questions asked*, I reminded myself. I'd do a recount when we made port before the handover. Hoping for storms, for the reckless abandonment of stock thrown overboard in the spray. Knowing so little of sailing on the open seas, I thought that it was then that I placed my life in its hands. Not back when I'd first stepped foot on her waters and said goodbye to the safety of solid ground. But what did I owe this crew? I was just a visitor there on the ship, and by the time we reached port, they would search for a name that no longer existed. Who was I to stand in the way of some stolen goods? Who knew what mouths they fed? It was none of my business—*no questions asked*.

"I won't stop you," I said. I noticed her gaze sharpen with the slightest tilt of her head.

"See, that's the problem with memory. It's not really your choice, is it? If someone wanted to find me, they could." *What?* I wanted to ask her. "What's your title?" she asked me instead.

"What does it matter?" I replied sharply. "I'm not loyal to this crew," I offered, hoping it was enough to buy my life back. She huffed out a low chuckle, weaving past me and back into the shadows.

"Who are you loyal to?" she called back from the dark.

I waited there until I could hear the familiar sounds of footsteps above me and the crew calling out to one another over the churning of the waves. *What just happened?*

It was then that I finally caught my breath. She was gone—just like she said she would—and I was still alive. *A chance. Disappear. Move on.*

I rushed back above deck in my panic, skipping steps and vision blurred in a hastened daze. I was so unravelled I nearly ran straight into an Exorci—unmistakable in her robes, the colour of charcoal left behind from their blaze.

"Careful," she said, catching me by the shoulders and stopping me in my flight.

"I'm so sorry," I spluttered and recoiled to collect myself.

She smiled a warm smile and lowered the hood of her black uniform, decorated with symmetrical golden embroidery of the greatest of all Exorci, and the source of the corruption in their image: Moultisjka the Terrible, immersed in the fires she made and forever crowning the heads of the individuals who inherited her power. Tabashi took such pride in dressing their greatest soldiers, in reminding everyone of why they're feared—descendants of the scourge.

"That's alright," she said, stepping back to give me space. "I'm Rimisin. It's a pleasure to meet you," she offered with her outstretched hand. Her face and her eyes were round and kind. She had unruly black hair slicked to her forehead in curls. But the rest of her hair she'd tamed into a long braid, draped over her shoulder and woven with a thin piece of blue string. "To remind me of home, Petakai," she answered perceptively.

"I'm Linh," I said sheepishly. "I'll be keeping a record of the stock. Sorry for—"

"Are you alright? You're very warm," she asked, despite standing some ways away from me. *Tamers of fire.* I imagined she must see heat—as we see colour, and perhaps as I saw the water.

"I—I thought I saw a rat," I blurted.

"Really? Would you like me to check? That's not good for a ship."

"No!" I exclaimed far too loudly. "It's alright, I didn't. I just thought I did. It's . . . my first time on a penjajap . . . or any ship, really." I sighed, my emotions buoyed by finally saying something true. "What about you?"

"I'm here to help escort the crew and cargo safely across the seas. It's not my first time on a ship," she replied, turning her attention back towards the waves. "Some believe we're the ones drawing the danger."

"Sorry—what is the danger?" I asked, doubting I even wanted an answer.

"The naga." I'd stopped walking. A chill crept up my spine with the cool breeze. Rimisin simply continued staring out at sea, the poise of a seasoned professional— or a soldier in war. "It has guarded the passage between Tabashi and Petakai well before we tried to cross it," she sighed, a memory washing over her and fading just as quickly. "We're in its waters now."

Though my body was still, my mind reeled at the thought of sailing straight through naga territory. I knew they existed, the guardians of the sea. But I thought we found them in the furthest reaches of Isira, in the distant lands of great adventurers, not here—just outside Tabashi's borders. What riches awaited us in Petakai that could be worth such a risky expedition?

"But hey, if we're lucky, there should be nothing to fear. There have been crossings before with no sightings. Let's hope for boring," she finished, offering me some reassurance. I followed her gaze out to a sky with a heavy sinking sun, easing its way into the evening. The colours of a sleepy afternoon washing over our tired bodies. The calm amongst the crew, despite the odds. The open ocean so gently brushed against the *Bayanihan*. It all looked and felt so peaceful. I couldn't imagine a danger in the deep the size of rivers—or so the legends were told.

✵✵ 6 ✵✵

I followed Rimisin for the rest of the afternoon, taking some comfort in her ease. Listening to the tales of her travels. She taught me which end of the ship was the stern and which was the bow, and who to ask for the strongest smelling salts, small packages of menthol and camphor providing a sharp scent to help keep one's head clear.

"So tell me, what would possess someone to board a penjajap meant for battling a naga?" Rimisin asked with cheer. So comfortable despite the danger. But I figured that's how they must have made it through, after all those years, across all those passages.

"Truth be told," I began, "I didn't know and I didn't want to ask. It all felt a little too easy, but I needed this job as much as you needed someone to sign up." I hoped Rimisin wouldn't press me further. Thankfully, she let me keep my secrets—as I had done with hers.

"The kunchuwarri they had on the docks brought us luck. They're a good omen apparently," she mused. "Do you think freeing the creature turns the tides in our favour?"

I simply shrugged; I was only ever taught about the magical world from our manuscripts, not from the writers themselves who would know the answers to such questions. We passed a sailor praying, kneeling by the balustrade, with a necklace of small wooden beads in their pressed palms. I asked Rimisin about preparing for the worst, thinking, *Now or never.*

"You want my advice? Nothing prepares you. I hate to tell you, but we've lost enough people to know that you either make it across or you don't." Her face darkened, and she turned away. That's why it had all been so easy. It didn't matter that I came without a title—because I was expendable. It was all a gamble then—but they must have spent a hefty sum on the construction of the ship, and I trusted that the *Bayanihan* and its loyal crew would not go down without a fight. There was some comfort in that.

"You'd be surprised," she continued, softening. "You've survived this long in Tabashi. I can't imagine the life you've had. You know more than you think, Linh."

The colours of the sunset bled onto the wood of the deck, giving it a soft, warm haze. I looked up to see that the sky itself was ablaze. Orange and pinks slowly faded into shades of purple as the night crept in from the horizon. I released a breath. I'd made it onto the ship, and we were bound for Petakai. Survive the seas. Then, when we reached port, the *Bayanihan* would regrettably lose their record keeper in the crowds. Stowaway or naga be damned, it was the *Bayanihan*'s problem and not mine. I shut my eyes to whisper my quiet prayer to Shi: *may your tides guide me.*

But before I knew it, I felt a shiver down my spine. I opened my eyes to a darkened sky. There was tension in the crew; an eerie silence had gripped them, with wary looks out to a murky view of the sea. The wind picked up, whipping my hair and clothes around me. The salty air bit at the corners of my eyelids, and I could taste the sharpness on my tongue.

"It shouldn't be this rocky so close to shore," Rimisin murmured, heavily resigned. I shot her a look of panic. Then I heard the crew stirring.

"Captain!" yelled the lookout from their position, hanging off the beam of the tallest sail.

"Here she comes!" shouted the captain. The *Bayanihan* rocked, battered by the biggest wave I'd felt so far. I raced with Rimisin to the edge of the deck and peered over the balustrade. A dark shadow snaked its way through the water. So large, I first mistook it for a shadow cast by the penjajap itself.

"Ready?" Rimisin called to me and threw a satchel for me to catch as she raced to the bow. "If it comes for you, use those. Call for me."

"What?" I cried out, stuck in place. Crew had rushed to their stations. Each one knew their part. I looked down and opened the bag; it was full of small silver rounds. What was I meant to do with those?

"Ready, Captain!" Rimisin called out to her. Another wave, and I lurched forward. I grabbed the bannister with my free hand and clung to the satchel as some rounds sprung out and scattered onto the deck.

"Ready the catapult . . . fire!" The captain ordered, and I turned to see a small projectile being launched out to sea. Then it burst into flames. I turned back to see Rimisin. Hands raised and paired with a gaze that was fixed on it.

Her black robes billowed in the uproar of the oncoming winds, and the waves charged against us—similarly inspired. I could have sworn that the embroidery on her robes glowed like the fight of a coal fire refusing to extinguish. In the swell of danger, another memory—one I had tried so hard to smother—threatened to burst back into my mind: an ox, a girl, and a terrible fire.

Another wave. Then a crash. The surface of the water broke, and the naga rose from it, the great serpent of the ocean. Its hiss was like the sound of a thousand snakes caught in the currents and summoning the tide. Its body an extension of the sea, impossibly tall against the backdrop of the setting sun. Its scales glowed a brilliant blue, with fins along its spine that fanned out like crystal daggers. It fell into the flaming barrel with its jaws open, consuming the fire.

"Get us out of here!" the captain yelled to Rimisin, and she obliged, swiftly turning her body to face the sails. She moved her arms in a circle around her until she grasped at an invisible rope tethered to them. She pulled, crying out with the strain of it, and our sails stretched to catch the wind she'd called. *Was the catapulted flame just a distraction?*

The *Bayanihan* lurched forward, and that time I fell, too slow to catch myself on the balustrade, spilling the bag and its contents onto the deck. *Shi have mercy*. I scurried to grab them all, impossibly difficult to see in the storm and slippery from the spray.

"It's coming back!" called out one of the crew from behind me. The *Bayanihan* shook violently as the naga slammed its tail into our hull with an incredible force that threw me down onto the deck. It knocked the wind out of my sails and I struggled to catch it back, watching as the chaos unfolded. The crew raced to arm themselves. They were preparing to fight it. *How?*

"Linh, head below deck!" Rimisin called out to me as the captain ordered the crew to—

"Ready another barrel!"

I crawled my way across the planks. Hands gripping onto what few silver rounds I had left.

"She's onto us!" someone yelled. Panicked shrieks from all around. I had almost made my way to the hatch for the shelter when I heard the rumble. A muffled gurgling beneath the tides. Oceans piled on top of each other and fought to climb. I stopped. Droplets of water started bouncing off the deck like rain falling backwards. I looked up to see the naga rising out of the deep. I thought it looked right at me. Great twin eyes of blue flame on the face of the ocean's dread, glowing far brighter than the stars in the night sky behind it. *Nothing prepares you, she'd said. By the grace of Shi, she was right.*

"Fire!"

I heard it that time, the catapult firing—like thunder from a gong. A blazing heap of material smashed into the side of the naga. It hissed. The chilling sound filled my ears. It all happened close enough for me to feel the heat of the flames. I smelled burning. The searing of flesh and the turning of water to steam. I felt powerful arms around me—Rimisin's. Pulling me to my feet as another barrel lit up. Another hiss. More like a scream. The creature shook itself from the flames and dove head-first into the sea. Sending a wave onto the *Bayanihan* and propelling us away from it. Rimisin let me go to pull at the wind again. She was struggling against the force.

Beneath the waves, barrelling towards us with god-like speed, the naga rose again—breaking through the tide with mouth agape. *The warning from the market.* Before me was a sky full of stars in the grip of razor-sharp teeth lining a fiendish wide grin. I threw whatever tiny silver rounds I had left towards it, crying out for Rimisin's help. I watched as the night fell towards me with terrifying speed. Then, before the stars could crash into me, I saw blinding crackles of light interrupting the sky. The silver rounds had broken apart into flashes of lightning that filled the air between me and the darkness that would have enveloped. The naga recoiled and readied itself for another plunge into the sea.

"It wants the witch!" someone cried out. Did they mean Rimisin? But she had just saved me.

"Then it can have her!" yelled the captain. The *Bayanihan* swung, and it threw Rimisin off balance. She slammed into the balustrade and buckled over it—falling.

"No!" I shrieked, a piercing sound. A child's scream. I reached for her when suddenly my mind shattered, flooding with the waves of a memory I could no longer hold back.

Shadow swallowed Rimisin's body as a new form took. Flames lit up the sky behind her and a giant black ox burst forth from the swirling inferno. I saw only her, my best friend. She was falling from me—again. The storm in her eyes so dark against the flames.

But I was reaching for Rimisin. I was reaching for her—the ox bellowed, its horns gleaming in the midnight sun. A thorny crown of ivory atop its hefty brow. Then, without warning, a burst. A terrible fire. It engulfed me. I felt myself flying, swirling past the skyline. Daylight into dusk, fading into the endless night. The last thing I remembered: eyes of flame, twin suns in the midst of the inferno. A million hands that reached back for me, a million times that I couldn't grasp them—couldn't save her.

Another burst.

The image shattered against me. A wave of water. Immeasurably cold and painfully real. The ocean engulfed me, rapids churning in my throat. Throwing me into the sunset. Stars into fire and back into the streaky horizon, like a wet painting turned over too soon. I was suffocating, slowly and breathlessly in the black sea. Sinking beneath the tide to rest against the giant palm of a hand on the seafloor. How was it possible that I had sunk so far down? I couldn't tell anymore what was real.

As I looked up, searching for the surface, I could almost make out features of a face—hers, a beautiful shade of the deep, smiling a warm mother's smile and staring back down at the broken thing she had to leave behind. The last thing I saw I was circling like the herons over a stormy ocean, looking out at the eyes of the sea, twin moons sinking beneath the tide.

** 7 **

I heard the shorebirds first. Then, a thought, *I am dead.*

But I soon felt the warmth of the early morning sun gently blanketing my cheek, buffering a cool breeze that wafted in with a whiff of the ocean. My bed was soft and plush, and I could hear the waves too, but far away. Drifting through the sensations, I tried to brush away at the mist that collected behind my eyelids. The stillness of my body told me I was no longer vessel-bound, floating on the open sea and at the mercy of its currents.

Daring myself to wake up, I was surprised to find my body surrounded by deep red silks and drapery. Gold and blue embroidered cushions on an ornately carved four-poster bed, each post with winding curves that twisted like vines up the trunk of a tree, reaching high into a silk canopy. I used whatever strength I had left in my fingers to trace the fringe of the cushions beside me—I'd never felt fringe before, let alone silk. My next thought was, *I am definitely dead.*

The polished wood was impossibly smooth, the carvings into it made with a careful hand to form tiny buds and blooming flowers surrounded by delicate leaves. What type of person could command such respect, and what was I doing in their bed? Shi must have welcomed all her creations with such luxury, letting them rest in warmth they've never known at the end of their arduous journey. Those were the eyes I must have seen before I closed my own.

But now, with mine open, they wandered to the walls of the bedroom—painted in exquisite detail with patterns and murals that stretched from the floor to the high ceilings. I was drawn into them. Wandering along with the stories they told. I didn't recognise the people or their faces. These stories weren't familiar to me. But then the image of a girl caught my attention. I recognised her likeness, and a name was formed—Rimisin. But if I was here, where was she?

The painful rush of memories pooled in to drown my mind with emotion—a flood, the *Bayanihan*, the naga. Rising from the bed as fast as I could—as slow as the sunrise—my body aching and stiff. I couldn't remember falling asleep. I couldn't remember anything. *How long have I been here? What happened?* I looked down to see that I was still wearing my clothes from when we boarded the *Bayanihan* in Tabashi. *Only yesterday*, I thought.

I climbed out of bed. It was like wrestling with dirt after they buried you under a mountain. My head felt heavy—full of dark rolling clouds catching on the peaks of thoughts that I couldn't quite form. I held onto the bedposts for support and looked out at the window to disperse the clouds with the morning sun. For a moment, they did.

Shimmering in the light outside was a brilliant sheet of sapphire blue, as deep as the night before the dawn and as bright as its breaking. I'd never seen the ocean from this high before. Then, another thought—a realisation: I'd never seen the ocean from this side of the map before.

A wide and glorious balcony opened out to a view of the ocean, and I felt myself float towards it, wanting to drift into the scene like the wind that beckoned.

"Quite the trick you pulled back there," I heard from beside me after I'd crossed the threshold. If I hadn't been so sluggish, the shock of it might have stopped my heart. I turned to see the stowaway perched on the bannister, legs dangling off the edge, playing with her machete. The very one she'd held to my throat. "So what are you?"

"I'm sorry?" I croaked. Feeling that same throat now immeasurably dry.

"Are you a spy?" she asked, tossing and catching the machete for fun. Holding it steady.

"I'm . . . a records keeper," I stuttered.

"Shi, what are they buying?" she chuckled. "How much are they paying you?"

"I don't know what you're talking about," I sighed, feeling myself fade. When I came to, I felt her arms around me—holding me up. I realised then that her face was no longer covered. I confirmed the colour of her eyes, her dark hair like the clouds in the sky before a storm. It was unbearably familiar—*what was her name again?*

"You've been asleep for three days. You need to eat," she said. I shoved myself away from her and stumbled back into the room.

"Three days? Where am I?" I demanded weakly. "And who are you?"

"To what do I owe the truth?" she replied easily.

"I'm . . . I'm not a spy. I answered a job posting for a records keeper on a penjajap bound for Petakai. Everything after goes dark," I snapped. "And you?"

She was silent. I shuffled to the door.

"It's locked," she said. "They're going to keep you until they know what you are, and what to do with you."

"And who are *they*?" I cried. My emotions crashed into me, relentlessly. I banged my fists into the door. Then, realising I was too weak to express the fullness of my rage, I rested my head against it—defeated.

Then I heard footsteps coming from outside. I spun to see that the stowaway had vanished just as the door swung open behind me.

"Praise Shi. You're awake."

"Rimisin!" I exclaimed the moment I caught sight of her, and she embraced me tightly. "I am so glad to see you're okay."

"Are you alright?"

"Yes, what happened?"

"They've been waiting to speak with you."

"Who?"

"The council."

"Tabashi's?" I pressed. Even in my dazed state, I felt myself seized by an urgent panic. Flashes of images pummelled my mind like droplets of the ocean cascading off the body of the naga. Faces of girls being dragged away in the night by the light of the Council's fires, thrown into ox-drawn carriages. Soldiers in service of their war. *The price of magic.*

"No, Linh. Petakai's council," she said finally, having searched my face. I felt the relief wash over me. "Linh, what do you remember?"

"Nothing," I admitted.

"Shi help us."

"Rimisin, tell me what happened," I begged, still feeling myself fade.

"I will. Can you walk? They're waiting," she assured me, her voice tender. She held her hands out to me and I took them gratefully—her touch was steadying.

We made our way across a long and winding balcony that overlooked the ocean. Seagulls circled in the breeze above us. Below them, the sea stretched out into the pale horizon, bright with the rising sun. The peaks of the waves catching the light before they dissipated back into the blue.

Rimisin told me about the night in fragments, her washes of memory in stark contrast to my own. In her eyes, I had never sunk. A commander of the tide, communing with the creature from the deep. "Impossible! I saw the bottom of the ocean," I attested, but she couldn't deny what she had seen with her own eyes, as much as I couldn't with mine.

When it was all over, I had fallen back onto the ship into a slumber that they could not wake me from. I tell it to you like this, Reader, because it was as much a tale for me as it is to you. Rimisin's account gave me no tether with which to lead me to the shores of my understanding. I was still adrift in my own memories, the eyes of the sea staring down at me, unblinking. I cannot deny what I saw then—or even now.

At the end of the balcony there were great towers that rose from the cliff side, ancient carved architecture as intricate as the bedposts and the murals in my bedroom, with spires capped in peaks of blue similar to the colour woven into Rimisin's braid. I watched the colour in her hair as it danced while she walked, so much more alive than the carved stone; those were as ancient a part of Petakai as the cliffside that rose from the shore. We continued in silence through a maze of corridors until we reached the doors to the meeting room. Rimisin's grip on my hand never faltered.

✳ ✳ 8 ✳ ✳

"Welcome, Linh of Tabashi, to Petakai."

Nalini Singh, leader of Petakai's council, addressed me from across a gleaming stone chamber. She wore a robe of deep maroon, embroidered with threads that looked like trapped starlight. Her curly black hair had been slicked into a neat bun at the nape and she'd decorated it with a striking gold necklace so intricate I mistook it for lace. Her face had been powdered with pigments to complement her dark complexion and she had outlined her angular features with brush strokes of gold, likened to the halls that she commanded.

Those halls were also impossibly beautiful. Angular patterns in long channels carved into the polished marble and filled in with gold. Lit candles flickered in the breeze from the open walls, their light catching on the rim of the chalices on the grand conference table running down the centre. Heavy cobalt curtains decorated the columns, framing the panoramic views of the entire ocean off the cliffside. We gathered here, up high. I didn't know I had a fear of it until then.

Nalini introduced the other members of Petakai's council. Nobles dressed in their finest, some from Petakai and others from Tabashi. A man in a robe of silver, gold hoops in his nose connected to the cuffs on his ears with fans that stretched out like an unfurled palm leaf. A woman in a shifting dress that rippled as she moved, coloured like the feathers of a peacock. She'd accessorised with silver chains and a headdress of white lace that fell behind her like a veil. One tall council member had seams up their robe like the bark of a tree—blossoming into the petals of a flower that curled around their collarbone.

I wondered again whether I was dead. But the looks that found me from across the table held no warmth, and so I let myself believe it was all real, and that I was definitely alive—lest that be my last resting place. I had thought of disappearing on these shores. To wander into the crowd that met us at the docks and find a new name to don myself with, and a new set of clothes to match, to learn about a world without strife and the constant threat of a cloudless sky above a thirsty field. But Petakai's council did not wear the face of leaders languishing in the laps of plenty. What trials could a well-fed kingdom face? So shut off from the rest of the map, in their own little corner of Isira. Perhaps if all you've known is riches, you can't help but want more.

As Nalini finished her introductions, she turned back to meet my gaze. I was on the other end of the hall, but she'd seized me with such conviction that I felt my body melt in the heat of her glare. I was momentarily robbed of my lies—the falsehood of my name.

"You've met our ship's captain, Captain Tanhchana Wardhani."

"I'm proud to command the *Bayanihan* in your waters, Nalini—"

"And her Exorci, Rimisin Azmi," Nalini continued, without missing a beat. She had no time to lose. "Rimisin went to great lengths to make sure you got the rest you needed."

I felt a squeeze in my hand.

"But you must understand our urgency, Linh. What happened on the crossing sits between our cities—"

"Nalini," the captain began again.

"You've said your piece."

"The waters are borderless."

"But your cargo is not."

"Linh is not cargo," Rimisin fired, and I reared from the heat of her words too. What had brought on such sympathy for me? I traced the stream back to that night. Was it her giving thanks for reaching for her? Had I earned her respect in attempting to do the impossible?

"She's a person," the captain said calmly. Rimisin and the captain shared a look. I remembered the captain almost throwing her overboard; such had been my cause for reaching. It seemed they had an understanding enough to conduct themselves for the meeting. I was grateful for that. Because as the meeting drew on, I realised the size of the chasm between those in my favour and those who were not, how the unfavourable outnumbered us.

"She's a person without a *title*," voiced a council member. Their tall body draped in bark made them appear like a towering tree in the marble forest of these immemorial beings.

"What is your full name, child?" the man in silver called out.

Reader, our kingdom did not have last names. Before this age, the title was what we used. It functioned similarly and connected you to your family's land, and thus your ancestry. Some titles were much more powerful than others—some bought, some gifted, some traded for. Perhaps I need not use it in this translation, and the last name would suffice, but "last" is not the word I would use to describe such things.

"She has a title. She belongs to Tabashi," called out a voice from behind a golden mask with a long trunk and a pair of tusks. They were a member of Petakai's council that represented Tabashi, one could assume from their looks, and I felt the room ignite in a furious response to their comment.

"Please!" I finally said above the growing disagreements, hoping that my voice could cut through the noise with the same strength of the captain's. It did not. But I kept trying. "I'm sorry, I need some kind of explanation—what is this all about?"

"Well, Linh of Tabashi," answered Nalini above the others, "in the water between our kingdoms, you brought down an ancient beast with magic we haven't seen in your lands for hundreds of years. So you'll forgive me for my tone, but it's *you* who has some explaining to do."

"For the pretty price on your head," the captain added coldly.

"Captain!" Nalini shot at her, a look of scorn.

"We could have died!" the captain shot back with equal force. "She has a right to know."

"Shi have mercy. Shall we shout out the window? Tell all of Petakai as well?"

The frankness shared between them took me by surprise. I guessed they were comfortable enough with each other to yell, or that there were no holds barred—given the gravity of the situation.

"The kid was on my ship," the captain said. "She's under my protection."

"I'll remind you, *pirate*, that the *Bayanihan* belongs to Petakai," the silver council member warned with seething venom, and his words struck a chord that rang out to silence the disquiet.

It was an incriminating insult, but one that seemed to affect no one else more than Nalini. I took in a quick breath, fearing that the fire of her anger could consume all the air left in the room—and that I would suffocate without it. *What did he mean by "pirate"? Who was the captain to Nalini?*

"Yet I was the only one brave enough to command it," the captain responded evenly, holding Nalini's gaze as she did.

I assumed the captain had earned her rank, but how long ago—and to whom did she owe that advantage? I slowly realised that there was a web in Petakai as old and interwoven as Tabashi's—the secrets of a kingdom that held up the toppling tide, climbing to reach it before its breaking point. But which would break first, and were we all just delaying the inevitable flood?

"Know your place," Nalini said with a quiet voice, and the room recoiled as if she'd shouted.

Seated, my gaze downcast in humility, I could spot the movements of Nalini's right hand that she had rested on the table. It was subtle—but intentional. I would have mistaken it for absentminded fidgeting, something that I can catch my own hands doing, until the captain's left hand made a similar gesture in return. *Were they communicating that way?*

After a long and tense silence, the silver council member spoke again. "This is beyond you, Captain." He turned to look at me. "For there is a great price on her head, and Tabashi will pay it."

So that was it then. Across the sea, yet there I was—in another room of people wondering where I had come from and deciding to whom I belonged. So much for starting anew, in a kingdom where at least the breeze didn't already know me by name. It seemed some things you can't outrun with brute force. The meeting of Petakai's council slowly faded from my listening ears as I watched the morning sun stream in and settle on the floor before me. I felt the warmth of Rimisin's hand in mine and patiently waited for it all to be over.

9

Off the shores of Tabashi and battling the naga I had performed a feat of magic to which everyone on the *Bayanihan* had borne witness except me, an Estari—the word bounced around the room like an echo. We'd once heard it in tandem with the Exorci, but only in our ancient history. They were the other magic users in Isira, blessed creations of Shi that held some ability to be in connection with her divine powers. Anamashta the Great was the last known Estari in Tabashi, and since the Great War—because of it—magic users were revered and despised in equal measure. To some people, we were abominations, sent to unmake the work of the creator and bring about devastation. This was a reputation that had held fast through the years thanks to the efforts of Moultisjka the Terrible. Because despite the Greatness of Anamashta, it was together that they brought on such destruction to the lands. If we cannot have one without the other, some believe we should have none.

Petakai's council believed that because I was on the penjajap that they'd paid for when my powers were discovered, they had some stake in its claim. A claim that I soon learned was much greater than power or magic; it was a claim to ancestry. But the penjajap had been built in Tabashi, by Tabashi's carpenters, in Tabashi's harbour. More importantly, I was *of* the kingdom, and so to the Council I would eventually return, with or without Petakai's stakeholders' hands around my wrists.

The meeting went on like that for longer than I cared to notice, so I spent the time adrift in my mind, trying to find a stream that would lead me to the night I couldn't remember properly—every current that met me was one of vivid imaginations and images without explanation. After they had all argued for a way to put a price on what was not theirs, the meeting was adjourned—with no decisions made. Before we all left the room, Nalini invited me to explore the city under Rimisin's watchful protection. We left silently, Rimisin barely acknowledging the captain.

"So you're my keeper now?" I asked her bitterly as we made our way down the corridor.

"We're all just following orders, Linh. Even Nalini," she said.

"Were you ordered to forgive the captain?" I challenged.

"Tanh will do what she must for her crew," she replied quickly.

Did she mean Tanhchana, the captain?

"Rimisin, how can you defend all this?" I blurted, the frustration clear.

"Call me Rimi," she said, and she stopped walking, turning to meet me in my plea. "Linh, I am sorry. But this . . . your magic . . . is bigger than all of it."

I recalled the murmurs. That I had brought the beast *down* with Estari magic. But what did that mean, and to what end? Even if I was an Estari, I surely wasn't the only one in all of Isira; I was just the only one born of Tabashi since the Great War. If water was so scarce and expensive, imagine how much more it would cost to employ the masters of the element. But what good could they really do in a kingdom suffering through a centuries-long drought? *Too many questions.*

"All I want, truly, is to keep you safe," Rimi finally spoke through gritted teeth, and I realised her hands had been bundled into fists. Power was hoarded in Tabashi, whether magical or economic, by the Council who sat on the throne in place of the king. If they discovered you had a gift that could turn the tides of war in your favour, then you would be taken to have it silenced or controlled.

* * *

Shrouded in darkness, after a child had shown their hand, they would come for them. The Council, in their decorated carriages. They used to ride during the day, hailing it as an honour: to be raised in the lap of luxury amongst the elite. But after centuries of parents watching their children being taken away to fight in other people's wars, their high regard turned to disgust. Parents stopped reporting their magical discoveries, and soon the Council had no choice but to take them by force—relying on informants. Though the villagers would prefer to use the term "rat." But our people were hungry, and maybe a life in the palace was a better one than what could be offered at home. Choices made when there seemed to be no others are always the choices that are regretted the most. No amount of coin given for a child can ever make the exchange not feel like a robbery.

I remembered that day that we spent in the Eyrell courtyard playing with sticks. Laughing uncontrollably after the grumbling noise that had erupted from my belly. We were just playing—until we heard the screaming. They were taking her away. Clawing at her captors with all her might, it didn't matter where she was going; that young girl was being taken from her friends and the only life she knew.

We watched in horror as she cried, unable to fight off the clawing hands of circumstance. We were sure we'd never seen her show any kind of magical capabilities. But the Council paid good coin for their young soldiers, and sometimes it didn't matter if they really had powers or not. If she could handle herself in a fight, then she could be part of the call to it. The best way to survive was to give no one a reason to fight you, or to come looking.

We stopped playing pretend after that day; all of us were as well-behaved as ever having finally learned the lesson of consequence. As they took her away, I seared her face into my mind. The Council changed the children's names sometimes so that the parents wouldn't go looking for them; they couldn't take them back even if they found them. But I would remember; I swore it. Linh, *of Tabashi*.

* * *

I searched Rimi's face for a sign of the memories—and the pain we may have shared—but she gave me only reassurance that she would see these Petakai council meetings by my side. I was grateful to have an ally and too tired to fight. She wore Tabashi's robes but Petakai's blue ribbon in her hair, and the resemblance of her kin. Maybe we could begin an exchange, starting with me telling her my real name, the both of us sharing real things about each other. But I hadn't yet given up on the idea of escaping. So, closing myself again—easily, as I always have—I replied, "Rimi, you must believe me. I'm no Estari."

The sound of a gong and bamboo flutes sung out, echoed through the waking city beyond the marble walls. There was music and laughter in the streets, and I could smell the aroma of freshly baked roti and delectable spices that wafted in from the markets. Though I was vaguely familiar with this cuisine, Tabashi once being a trading city and having welcomed many foods and cultures, there is nothing better than tasting recipes from their birthplace.

"Shall we? Take our mind off it for a bit?" Rimi asked—hopeful. I smiled back at her. She needed this too.

Petakai unfurled from the wide-open doors of the building we stepped out of. The kingdom's magnificence in busy neighbourhoods with elaborate multi-storied residences—beautiful pavilions painted in shades of blue with carved arched doorways, paired with bright orange window panes opening out to the sunshine. From where we were on the steps of the cliffside, we could almost see the entire island, the mountainous terrain on which it sat. To behold an entire kingdom in one sweep, one that I had once only dreamed of reaching across the sea, was the feeling I wished to share with the one person who wasn't there. But despite it all, I could feel proud. I had made it across, almost free. If only I could have brought her with me.

Rimi grabbed my hand, and we made our way down to the stalls. The air was thick with the heady aroma of clove and chilli and the tang of freshly caught seafood. As we walked through the alleyways, I let myself get lost in the vibrancy, the novelty of it all. Intricate patterns on silks and hand-carved wooden trinkets by hanging plates of embossed silver.

"Exorci! Over here!" I heard in the crowd and turned to see a drunken woman, swaying with her drink still in hand. She held up her loose sarong that was haphazardly tied to her body, but her behaviour didn't garner any extra attention above the rest; the streets were already a riot of excitement. Her dialect intrigued me; I couldn't tell if it was a speech slurred by her drink or by her tongue. Rimi's gaze was noticeably fixed on the way ahead.

"There's an unlit hearth in my home for your pretty powers!" the woman sneered as we continued on our path. I heard snickers from the crowd.

I tried to catch the expression on Rimi's face, to offer some sympathies with mine, but she was masked from my view. It seemed no matter where we went, Exorci would be treated with some kind of hostility. I remembered revering them, thinking there could be nothing greater. Then I grew up—learned that the world did not take kindly to precious things. That a rare gift could draw wonder just as easily as it could a target on one's back. Often it's the silent who survive.

"Is it no different in Petakai then?" I asked Rimi, once we had cleared the noise.

"A little. Exorci help in the mines and don't threaten the fields," she replied with a sigh, "so we get some mercy for that."

We walked past a stable. Tied to the posts were a group of saddled kikiriki, idle beside their stable master. I immediately stopped in my tracks. Their blue feathered bodies shivered with the breeze, with red scaly legs that ended in sharp talons gripping onto the dirt, and a neck that rose high above the height of their master, ending in a long golden beak glistening in the sunlight—such was my cause for stopping. We had these creatures back in Tabashi. They were a preferred transport for those seeking a swift passage across the land because of the bird's impressive speed. But Tabashi's kikiriki heads had no long golden beak. Instead, their feathers gradually faded into a rough grey texture, eventually forming a tusked trunk—resembling those of a baby elephant. Enticed, I checked for the stable master's permission before I reached my hand out to stroke the bird.

Thunder cracked behind me—far too close for comfort in the middle of a cloudless day. The source of the noise was in a clearing, the centre of a gathered crowd, just outside the marketplace. There stood a tall and handsome man dressed in finely embroidered robes—boasting the colours of the kingdom. He held out his hands to reveal a small blue parcel tied with a single black string. He gestured for the crowd to pay attention, reached his arm up, then threw the parcel down onto the ground with such force as to shatter it. In an instant, a great bang rang out, the parcel lit up, and colourful and crackling flames danced from where the package had broken apart. The crowd similarly burst with excitement. It reminded me of the silver rounds that Rimi had handed to me on the ship.

"Again!" demanded the crowd, and the man gleefully obliged, pulling out another parcel from his pockets.

"Always the show-off," muttered Rimi under her breath.

"You know him?" I asked incredulously.

"Alewic Azmi, one of Petakai's brilliant scientists."

Azmi? I thought.

"Rimi!" the man called out, spotting us in the crowd and making his way towards us.

"My dad," she answered.

Beaming, Rimi ran to embrace him.

✷ ✷ 10 ✷ ✷

"We call them fireworks. Because of how it spreads, and the colours," Alewic said, grinning. He spoke with a soft voice that complemented the creases around his smile, framed by his glorious greying beard. His ears were long—a sign of the wisest of people and the goodness of their hearts.

Alewic had invited us back to his workshop, a charming and cluttered hut with limited headroom perched atop a hill just outside the city centre. Decorating the tables were empty vials and potions with drawings scattered across the walls and floor, signed with the scribblings of a genius. Behind us, a colourful glazed circular window looked out into an overgrown garden, its leaves rustled by the breeze brought in from the shore. The light that filtered in through the mosaic image of Shi rested on the empty mugs of tea and coffee left strewn about the place or stacked on bowls.

Alewic had filled every blank space in the workshop with charcoal drawings and calculations, even glueing crumpled paper to the walls—to make space for more. I had never seen so much paper before, let alone the hundreds found bound up in his many books. I marvelled at their construction, so used to only using palm leaf manuscripts or occasionally reading the inscriptions hammered into metal sheets.

"What have I told you about staying in here all day?" Rimi remarked, making quick work of retrieving some of her father's dishes with a joy that betrayed her tone. I thought about the many crossings she must have made without him. It was probably nice to come back and see that not much had really changed, and that she would always have a role to play in his life, as he did hers.

In his workshop, Alewic studied and refined the components for the fireworks. He presented me with a vial containing a black powdery substance. It was a combination of different powders, each with their own properties.

"What's incredible is the amount of energy stored in something so small and visibly unremarkable," he explained, gathering some rocks to show me. "The crude substances are completely harmless. We had to discover how to purify them—and then we had to figure out what amounts created the best results. It was very dangerous in the early days of experimentation."

I picked up a rock as Alewic brought the black powder over to a lit candle. He sprinkled the smallest amount into the open flame. It caused a flurry of sparks that brought about a flurry of delighted giggles. He spoke of saltpetre—a white powder in its pure form, and the most important in the mixture.

"Why have I never seen fireworks before?" I asked, exhilarated, turning over the rock as if it were a jewel.

"It's a relatively new science, but now everyone in Isira is trying to mine the materials and refine the manufacturing process. For hundreds of years our people thought saltpetre had no use, being inoffensive where it naturally occurs," he replied, holding up a rock similar to the one in my hand. "Petakai used to only have a penchant for pretty things from the mines."

"But it's not even mined in the traditional sense," Rimi said. "They collect saltpetre from the built-up bat guano on the floor of the caves."

I dropped the rock.

"What?" I cut in, thinking I'd misheard her.

"It's true! For years we've been walking right over the riches. It took my dad's genius to unlock its secrets, perfecting the purification process," Rimi clarified, leaning herself against a toppling tower of books in the corner.

"By accident—and not alone. It was your experiment, Rimi; don't forget that!" Alewic countered with pride. "The fun part is that it all comes down to the ratios: how much of which substance you need to create a rapid burn for an impressive explosion."

* * *

Deep beneath the island, in an extensive network of tunnels that snaked their way under the ocean, lay the mines of Petakai. The entrances were situated high on the cliffs that towered above the island's shores. Materials mined from these caves were brought down to the markets and shipped off to all neighbouring islands and kingdoms that sail could reach. In those caves where the air was rich with flammable substance, even the sparks from the pickaxes could set the whole strip alight. Exorci were stationed in the mines in hopes that they could control the flames—just long enough for the miners to escape a collapsing tunnel.

Alewic told me how, for centuries, Petakai had built its wealth through trade. Their island thrived, but it was only an island, and Tabashi had once served as their major gateway to the mainland. In the past, their alliance turned them into the most prosperous powerhouse in all of Isira. They welcomed ships into their harbour from all other kingdoms, both near and distant. There had even been a path through the Jungle once, connecting Tabashi to the north, to Lenfol, but that was centuries ago.

As Alewic spoke of all this, I thought about how big the world seemed and how small I was in the face of it all. I could recall all those lessons discussing the politics and economics of Isira. How I always found myself drawn to the stories instead. Imagining myself running off to tame the beasts of the Jungle, or swimming in the channels with the tigers that could breathe underwater.

"How do you know so much about Tabashi?" I asked Alewic, trying to catch his attention in between his tales.

"Well, I used to work there," he admitted. "I'm quite fond of it, actually. I'd like to return there one day. You'll have to come visit me when I do," he finished, and my mind clouded. How could I tell him that my plan was not to return—if I could help it?

There hadn't been a moment to slip away unnoticed. I would have to examine the open balcony of my room that night if there were no other options. With the kikiriki we spotted, perhaps I could get far enough into the island to lose any pursuers. I was sure Petakai's council could find another Estari to do their bidding. But the more Alewic spoke, the smaller the island felt—and so too my chance of escaping those who would come looking. I felt like I was being tossed around like grain, at the mercy not of the hands of the people who tended to it but those who sat in marbled halls deciding the labour's worth. It filled me with the fires that raged in Rimi earlier that day; we were more than soldiers, more than cargo, and at least we had each other to understand that.

Over the afternoon, Alewic showed me how to mix the powders and how to shape and mould the compounds. Even how to improvise with whatever materials I had. When he told me I could urinate on a bed of straw and wood ash, I thought he might have gone mad. He said it could be useful information to know if I was ever in a pinch and needed to escape. He didn't know how seriously I listened and how eagerly I took notes. I studied Alewic's teachings more than I'd ever done in school. It's not that I didn't enjoy learning; I just had objections to how things were taught. There is no better water to drink than from the source.

The Azmis were not unfamiliar with institutions for education. Their family were the inheritors of a substantial fortune from the founding of Vatthana University, built in Petakai after the Great War, by Vatthana Azmi. I had hoped to visit it during my stay in Petakai, however long it was going to be, but I regretfully missed out on getting a tour of the esteemed establishment by its own great-grand-inheritors.

"It's a wonderful university that is sadly missing my daughter's brilliant contributions," Alewic added at the end of his impassioned speech about its vast libraries.

"Dad," Rimi groaned in response.

"I know I can't convince you to go back."

"I still read, you know!" she exclaimed.

"It's not your mind I'm worried about, darling. I am just sorry for everyone else's," he finished, inspiring both of their laughs. A part of me wished to be privy to the memories they shared—they seemed much brighter than mine.

Alewic later brought out the blueprints for intricately designed devices that could launch projectiles out of a barrel with deadly accuracy—a type of weapon, some of them small and some much, much larger: firearms, aptly named. But these ideas and designs were all new to me, and I couldn't believe how trusting he was with the information—a trait he shared with his daughter—and I was simply grateful for their company.

"I've tried many times to convince my father to focus on these stronger weapons," Rimi added, having settled back into the space she'd always known, "with these designs we could—"

"I don't believe in violence," Alewic said quickly, with a sting, the first sharpness I'd detected in his voice since arriving at the workshop. "My work isn't in improving their danger; it's in making them safe. It's hard enough watching you sail off every few seasons—"

"On ships made safer because of your designs!" she cried.

"That's enough," he said with that same edge. In the silence that followed, Alewic softened. "Anger is a wound that festers and never closes. If you do not heal it, you won't die by fighting but by bleeding out." Rimi stormed out of the room. I watched as Alewic sighed into the emptiness she left. "Please forgive me and my daughter. It's not been the same since her mother passed. She was much better at these things."

"I'm so sorry," I whispered, suddenly feeling myself taking up too much space, and retrieved some of the sprawled drawings to return the workshop to the state we'd found it in.

"I was working in Tabashi. Rimi's mother would visit as often as she could to bring me supplies from Petakai," he said solemnly.

"Was she an Exorci?" I asked.

"No, no. Just a passenger. It was Rimi who fought to have Exorci travel with the ships . . . from that point on." And so I understood. Rimi had yet to explain to me her path in becoming an Exorci, but I could now guess at its ache. At least she had Alewic—and once her mother too. Someone who would have fought for her name to be remembered.

"The catapults and firebombs on the *Bayanihan*, were those her ideas as well?" I asked quickly, wanting to change the subject.

"A compromise. Rimi wanted my cannons on the penjajap. A new design, barely tested. But the projectiles for cannons are heavy and their material requirements are great. With the powers of an Exorci, we save on all that weight," he explained, taking me over to another table with paper spread out across it. He could so quickly submerge his mind into his work, distracting himself from reminiscing about the past. I could spot the behaviour because it was familiar.

"The naga seem to be drawn to fire," he said, "so we fill a container with enough material to make a big one, and then we launch it out to sea with a catapult. An Exorci can light it from afar."

"It's amazing, truly. I saw it in action. Is it harmless?"

"It must hurt the creature, but we cannot hope to kill it," he said seriously.

"Is it still alive?" I asked suddenly, seeing confusion spread across his face.

"You don't . . . remember?" he asked me in return.

"Everyone remembers a different version of events, including me." I sighed. Alewic stood up tall and leaned over, resting a hand on mine.

"Linh, I nearly lost my daughter the same way I lost her mother—and I have you to thank for bringing her home. We are forever in your debt."

* * *

I spent the rest of my first afternoon in Petakai in Alewic's workshop. Between the gently brewed chai and his mythical tales, their profound whimsy, I found a certain kind of peace. Anytime Alewic seemed to slow his thoughts to a trickle, I would ask another question that would inspire a waterfall. Rimi eventually returned. She had brought with her some skewered snacks from the markets and a spare change of clothes for me.

Alewic never again mentioned Rimi's mother, but he also never stopped smiling. How was it that he'd found his peace, and when was it that he'd found it? How long had it taken him? Had he travelled back to Tabashi for it? To seek a new life perhaps? *A chance to disappear and move on.*

"What do you know about Moultisjka the Terrible?" I asked, placing my teacup back on its tray with a delicate clink.

"The Terrible?" he repeated, holding back a laugh. I wondered how those stories were told in Petakai and whether the distance from the shores of the danger had tempered its threat.

"Sometimes we tell children these stories because of the threads of truth within them. They're tales of caution," he countered with a different tone to his previous warmth. "The powers of Shi have always been about balance. Everything I know about magic and about science asks the same."

"And Anamashta?" I asked, hearing the words "the Great" in my head. "Was she sent to balance Moultisjka?"

"Perhaps," Alewic replied evenly. I thought for a long time before asking my next question.

"Alewic, can you teach me how to use magic?"

✶✶ 11 ✶✶

"Powers. Of. Shi. It is not up to us to decide. If Linh's gifts come from her ancestors, then we honour that connection," Rimi sighed with controlled defiance as she paced across from Nalini. It was a beautiful new day in Petakai. Yet there we were, standing in the shaded halls, having the same argument as the days before. Since last night I couldn't climb out of the balcony and survive a fall off the cliff, I was there too. The entire room tensed, awaiting a response to Rimi's words.

I had slowly come to understand Rimi's position after all those conversations, the fires from which she flared. She didn't just speak for me, but she spoke for all magic users across all kingdoms—the ones whose lives were tossed and turned, subject to the whim of leaders who used people like cattle to execute their power.

I wished to offer more to temper the council, but I could not unsee the eyes of the ocean that had stared back at me from the bottom. Nothing else that I was told about that night had felt as real as those eyes. There had only been one other time in my life when I had experienced such a vivid dream only to wake days later—alone in a bed I didn't recognise. It was the day my memories all ended in flames. I should have known that the Council would come back, looking for the right girl. They should have known she would not go without a fight. There are only fragments of my visions that remained: the ox as black as coal; a fire like flying into the centre of the sun; a pair of storm clouds that stared back at me with a hand outstretched—one I couldn't grasp.

Not wanting to stay in that meeting room any longer than I had to, I swam back towards Alewic's workshop right after I had asked him about teaching me magic. Alewic didn't know how to help me; he had never met an Estari. Even though he had a hand in helping Rimi discover her powers, to avoid her lighting up the workshop with her excitement, Alewic could only tell me of the magic of an ancient one—the greatest one: Anamashta.

Be careful of the stories you hear, Linh, I heard in the waters of my mind, *and even more careful of the ones you write. You don't know who you exile with your words. Sentences are powerful decrees.*

His face faded from view. Flutters of memories lost to the setting sun and the rise of a new day. I would have a habit of flipping back the pages, trying to discover something I missed. A detail that could have changed things, some information that was the key. Or perhaps I was searching for a hand outstretched, promising myself that this time I would be ready to grasp it.

"And what about debt?" Nalini's sharp tone brought me back into the meeting room. "What of the ships we've sunk? The people we've lost? Trying to honour a connection to Tabashi from centuries ago."

The alliance that Alewic had spoken of. When the seas were safer and the ships could make the passage without event. What had happened between the kingdoms since then? Was this all really just about sunken barrels of rice wine?

"There's no alliance now, only payment," another council member snarled. "What do her ancestors say to that?"

"We have our own people to feed," Nalini finished. She would not falter from her position, even when pressed by the representatives of Tabashi. They argued this way for a long time, sometimes in harsh tones and raised voices but mostly, painfully, in silence.

"Understand this," Nalini said after some time, composing herself and turning to face Rimi and the captain. I sat up straighter in my seat. "Either we make a deal or you sail back to Tabashi for the last time."

* * *

Petakai had been my means of escape. It had become my prison—and to Tabashi we would eventually return if Petakai's council had anything to say about it. In my dreams, this was the kingdom to which all oceans led. Awake, it was just another kingdom on the map, surrounded by oceans or jungles, filled with their secrets and their beasts. It felt strange to be fighting so hard for the voice of a kingdom to which I felt no loyalty, but standing on the side of Tabashi felt like standing for freedom of any kind. In hindsight, this was a veiled attempt in those rooms. But the effort unlocked a belief in myself about the right way to do things I wouldn't soon forget.

"So why not then? Honour the connection?" a voice rang out from the other end of the hall.

"What?" shot Nalini, her pleasantries dropped. I couldn't imagine the bill these meetings racked up, the people who watched her. Can you have sympathy for the rich? The positions they stood in because of the choices they made. They gathered in a huddle outside of our earshot. I tried to make sense of the murmurs that I could make out.

"What are you saying? We can't discuss that here."

"That's another conversation entirely."

"It would take a hundred penjajaps to pay off their debt."

"They owe us more than they're worth."

"We'd be doing them a favour."

I felt them looking over at me, demanding satisfaction. Nalini motioned to a guard, and they ushered us out of the room where our names remained.

With the doors shut behind us and the hallways that loomed, the captain let out an exasperated sigh, banging her fist against the wall before turning to leave. The sound of her footsteps echoed as she walked, and Rimi and I raced to catch up with them. Guards flanked either side of us anywhere we turned.

"Nalini Singh and her endless stubbornness!" the captain cried out into the fire-lit halls, and I turned to witness the setting sun beside us out on the open balconies. I took a moment to pause and take it all in, perhaps for the last time. I was going to leave, and it would have to be soon.

"Second only to yours, Captain," Rimi replied steadily.

"The penjajap that Tabashi built worked. They should just order more penjajaps!" the captain said.

"The penjajap worked because Linh was on it," Rimi corrected.

"She gets one promotion and suddenly everything's money!"

"Coming from a pirate."

"Retired pirate, and don't call me that."

"Or what, you'll throw me overboard?" Rimi teased, but she could not hold back the bitterness that rose. They'd stopped walking. Her words stung like the scent that hung in the air: burning wood, old incense, and charred metal mixed with the unmistakable tang of sweat.

I held my breath, afraid to break the stillness as they stood locked in a silent battle of pride. Finally, Rimi broke it and walked away, leaving behind an uneasy calm that was almost as sour. The captain turned to me, her face keeping her secrets like one of Alewic's many well-bound books.

"Get a good sleep if you can, kid. Whatever their decision, we leave in the morning," she said and made her way back to her room.

"For the last time?" I called out to the back of her head, thinking of Alewic. Of his wish to sail back to Tabashi. Of my wish not to. I wondered if he could—if I could.

The captain barely turned to look at me when she replied, "Whatever their decision."

✳ ✳ 12 ✳ ✳

I retired to my room, noticing the guards lining the halls as I entered. But I knew that rest would not find me that evening, so I made better use of the time. They would lock the doors to my room from the outside. But the windows weren't locked—a small kindness.

It was time for a new plan. I retrieved the glass beside my bedside, its contents: fresh spring water for me to drink. They had patterned the vase with a single chain of sapphire blue around the neck with dimples from the handmade craftsmanship. I'd never held a glass vase before until that day. Looking down, I pictured the hands that had crafted it. Felt them climbing up my body. Moulding me into a product to be shipped off and sold to the highest bidder. I had to shake them off to concentrate.

Bringing the vase with me to the centre of the room, I held it out with the balcony in front of me and concentrated. I tried to summon a thing I'd only ever felt as shivers. A break from the days. Games we used to play. How do you learn to control the storms? I tried to do so by drowning them out, listening to the crash of the waves before me, calling to them with a quiet voice. I imagined the tide washing over me. In the silence, I sank and willed the ocean to push me back up. But nothing happened. So I tried again. Fighting for one more chance to get out. A slim possibility, receding like the tide. I thought of the *Bayanihan*, of the attack. Felt the heat rise. Hands grasping at me. Linh, taken. Rimisin, almost thrown into the dark sea. The scream rising in my throat just as I had that night, like a hole in my chest held open—I felt it surge. The glass vase shattered; the sound was sharp and cutting. Water cascaded down in front of me.

"Powers of Shi," I heard ahead, and looked up to see her—the stowaway.

"I'll call the guards," I lied.

"There's no need for that. I just want to help," she said, the sincerity in her voice coming as a shock to me. "I bet they haven't told you."

"Told me what?" I demanded.

"You're to be married. To the crown prince of Petakai. To pay off Tabashi's debts," she said.

My mind emptied. I did not know what to think. I felt something stale in my mouth. It was impressive how valuable my powers seemed to be. If I should have felt anger, I couldn't find it. That anger wasn't new at all—it was an old wound, one that I had padded with years and years of fighting and fleeing. Between villages, between jobs. It was almost a relief. Perhaps something I had always wanted. *A chance for a fresh start. A chance to disappear. A chance to move on.*

"Royal life. Not bad for a girl with no title," she said.

"What do you know about it?" I snapped. The tides crashing.

"I know you're lying," she toyed. "Tell me, what are you doing with a dead girl's name in your mouth?"

Fear took me. How could she have known? I thought about the fire, that fateful day at the Eyrell. Our names were never gossip in the villages, convenient for those who needed the children to have disappeared with the flames. How else could they explain what had really happened?

"She could be anyone," I said defensively.

"She could, but your response says otherwise," the stowaway teased, and I held my breath. I realised she was testing me, and I had no obligation to answer to another criminal. There could be no honour amongst thieves. In that moment we sized each other up, and I could hear the both of us asking the other in the silence: *what else are you hiding?*

"Want some help?" she asked, motioning to the water pooled at my feet, the shards of glass scattered around me. I felt caught in the swell of unanswered questions. A thunderous cloud roared—but I sighed and willed myself to tame them, bending to pick up the glass.

"There is energy all around us," I heard her say. She walked towards me, retrieving a small branch from behind her back that had been tucked into her waistband. "Magic seeks to wrestle with the inner workings of the world. We cannot create something new; we live in a closed system. Everything we need is already there. We just have to move it from one place to another."

She stopped a few breaths in front of me, held out the branch, and caught fire with it. So she was an Exorci, but not for the kingdom; she didn't wear their robes. I should have been searching for answers, but I was so distracted by the fire she'd conjured. I'd never seen it happen so clearly before; the air sucked in around the branch. I saw it turn into itself, and then into a flame. *Real magic*, right there in front of me. That little girl who loved to read couldn't help but smile.

"Why are you helping me?" I asked quietly, wondering why it had taken me so long to.

"I'm helping the future of Tabashi," she said boldly. Her answer caught me off guard. It was one thing to be belittled for having no title, to have your life laid out for you by people in marbled halls who do not know your suffering. *Future of Tabashi? Did she really mean that?*

"Okay." I recoiled, confused. "What concern is the future of Tabashi to you?"

Her eyes met mine, and I held my breath. I didn't know what she wanted from me, and in that infinite moment, I wanted nothing more than to find out.

"Look, I'm no Estari," she whispered, "but what I know is heat. I feel it all around me. I feel where it can flow, and I pull it to where it is not." She carefully took my hand and placed it under hers. "Find the fire; cool it down."

I took in a shaky breath. Against my better judgement, I closed my eyes and let the storm roll in. I saw their faces, heard their voices, the names that pulled me, my body like water, poured into vases shaped by others' hands. Thrown and shattering like the waves that broke against the rocks below. I thought of the sea, battering against the walls it came across. Relentlessly, incessantly free; the vastness of it all. Sinking deeper and deeper beneath the tide until I couldn't feel the swell. Until I found them—felt them—swimming around the room like rivers on the map, currents through the air. I caught one, letting it take me to where it pooled at the water by my feet, then to where the water wasn't. My name was on the breeze, being called out like a memory.

I opened my eyes.

Floating all around us were tiny droplets in the air, *like rain falling backwards.* But this was my magic, water that came to my calling. Circling around the flame, from one place to another, I willed them to it. Watched as the water mixed with the fire; watched them dance until it was all gone—fire and water, found.

A loud knock.

"Linh, are you alright?" I heard from Rimi through the door, and my head snapped that way in response. I felt a chill. It rushed in like the tide. I looked back to see that the stowaway had gone. Then, in an instant, Rimi was in the room. "The guards came and woke me. They heard a noise. Are you alone?"

"Yes," I answered, a little breathlessly. Rimi was eyeing the broken glass by my feet.

"Are you hurt?" she asked, concerned.

"No, it was just an accident. I couldn't sleep," I replied. Something true, the best way to lie. "Why didn't the guards come in sooner?"

She averted her eyes from mine.

"I didn't want to have to tell you, but . . . they're somewhat afraid. Rumours spread faster than truth, you understand?"

I nodded slowly and turned away from her to hide my embarrassment.

"Don't think too hard about it, Linh," she said. "They're wrong. Please try to get some rest—your body needs it. I will have someone clean up the mess in the morning."

"Rimi," I replied, "I've been asleep for three days straight. I don't need rest. I need answers."

✲✲ 13 ✲✲

As dawn broke, armoured soldiers addressed me with the news of our departure. Petakai's council had given me new garments for the entirety of my stay. So unused to the luxury, I had offered to return them in the morning before I got dressed in my last outfit. But they wanted me to look my finest on my return to Tabashi, gifting me with a beautifully bound leather case for my new belongings. A maiden came with the soldiers to remain with me in my room, assisting me with the morning's preparations.

I was told to cleanse myself with the basin of warm water provided, infused with the fragrant oils of jasmine and marigold flowers, as new garments made of rich and glorious silks were presented to me, gold embellishments decorating their hem. I enjoyed a breakfast they brought to my room, helping myself to various curries and roti and satay with spiced oils, all surrounding a heap of steaming fragrant jasmine rice. Some of those dishes I had tried back in Tabashi. But there, in the cradle of its origin, I beheld the flavours to their full potential.

Though my journey was fraught, I would not soon forget the simple pleasures, the moments that I would miss: Alewic's stories, shared in his workshop; touring the markets with Rimi; a stolen moment with a stowaway, the thought rising to redden my cheeks. I shook my head to focus. What I had learned in my few days in Petakai was that there would be no corner of the map that I could escape to where I wouldn't find a kingdom with a claim—to land, title, or people.

* * *

After bathing and dressing, I was ushered out of my room to join the gathering procession as we made our way through unfamiliar halls and up many more flights of spiralling stairs. How naïve of me to think that the rooms I'd already found myself in were the height of sophistication; here in the halls of the regent, the silks were deeper, the paintings brighter, and the marble so polished that the gold inlays appeared like freshly poured liquid metal, spilling away from their gilded frames. It was a sterile affair, attended by the guards and influential members of the aristocracy, Nalini included. This was not for a ceremony of marriage; this was purely so the royal family could look at—and approve of—the arrangement.

He looked young, the prince—and woefully indifferent. Prince Tamaravati. His family revered. They were equally passive as they sat silently beside him. After some time, his father, the king of Petakai, gave an inconspicuous nod. His crown tilted ever so slightly with him. It signalled the end of the audience. So, with that, we took our leave.

I was led to the docks and left to prepare for departure. Watched, always—I checked. Though I thought I might try for one last time to slip by unnoticed, every time I turned my head to check for openings, I found a watchful pair of eyes barring my path. In the past, I had never been someone worth paying attention to; disappearing was easy when no one was really looking. But now, as a captive and a commodity, I was a valuable treasure in a kingdom renowned for its prized possessions. I resigned myself to the fate that had been set before me.

When you find yourself pulled into the swell, your first instinct is to swim against the current, fighting with all your might against it. But this only serves to tire you out, worsening your chances of escape, and you may succumb to the sea. Sometimes the best way to escape it is to let yourself be pulled in by the whirl until the calm, when you have a better chance of swimming back to shore. With patience, I could bide my time. Waiting for the right moment, when I could break free from the confines of a life I didn't choose, to set out on one I could.

* * *

The shorebird cawed. Fishers waved. But this time, there were no captured kunchuwarri for the captain to liberate. I saw how easily she slipped back into her role, much more confident and comfortable at the stern of her ship shouting orders. The *Bayanihan* bobbed in the water, and she was as majestic as she'd been on Tabashi's shores; though she had a few more dings that needed oiling and patching. The crew were back in their usual routines, double-checking the rigging and tying up loose ends.

I had tried to approach Rimi in the quieter moments of the morning; I wanted to continue our discussion from the night before, or at least ask her about what had happened between her and the captain after the attack, but she dismissed me silently, busy with her own urgent business to attend to. She did use the opportunity to slip me a small sheathed blade, the exchange hidden in the sleeves of our garments and communicated with only a glance. The weapon was easily concealed, even in the purely decorative ensemble of my attire, its handle wrapped in well-worn leather, the only distinguishable feature being a small round sapphire embedded in the hilt, a perfect match to the thread in Rimi's hair. She must have trusted me, and feared for me. Despite the orders that she was following, Rimi was the type of person who would always lead with her heart.

I rolled my shoulders, feeling a knot between them that had been there since I had woken up. I couldn't tell if it was from the restless sleep, tossing and turning in my bed, or from the awkward hunched position I had found myself in when I finally got some. It was a three days' long journey back to Tabashi, and I didn't know how long the journey felt, given that I had been asleep for most of the first crossing.

Wanting to stretch my legs and familiarise myself with the *Bayanihan* once more, before I traded my balance for tolerance of the tides, I sought to distract myself with a simple occupation, making my way onto the *Bayanihan* and back below deck, seeking refuge in the records of stock. The rest of my journey would be uncertain, but in numbers, I might again find some peace. Admittedly, I also did not know what else I should do. It shouldn't have come as a surprise, but despite the news of our successful crossing—with no casualties from the attack—there were still no new sign-ups for the position that had brought me here. It was funny; in the most expensive clothes I'd ever worn, I started doing the work of the job I had taken when I had no money to my name and no other options.

Checking the numbers we had traded for against those we had departed with, I noticed a slight discrepancy, and red flashed across my memory. So much for finding certainty in numbers. I took note to blame the rough seas for the missing stock, or my lack of experience, increased prices for trade, a miscount. In a panic, I tore up the palm leaves, replacing them with numbers that I could explain. When I was done—surprised by how the task had rendered me breathless—I wandered about below deck, retracing the steps I had taken when I had first run into her, the stowaway. Then, realising what I was doing—that I was still searching for someone—I cursed myself for being stuck in my old ways. A kingdom away and I could not shake the habit.

"That's the last of it. Make sure it's secure," I heard from above me. "Let's get out of here."

As I gathered my thoughts, I realised I had wanted a goodbye; it was time to let go of my search. I wondered where the stowaway had gone, where her journey in Petakai would take her. I hoped that the world would be kind to her, that the goods she'd stolen would matter and save her from the pain of scarcity she must have also always known in Tabashi. As I made my way above deck, deep in my own rivers, I came face to face with Nalini Singh.

"Linh," she said, addressing me evenly as she stepped on board, luggage in tow. I raised an eyebrow.

"Cast off the lines!" the captain called, and I felt the familiar sensation of the *Bayanihan* bouncing on the waves, finally untethered to the shore—and with it any chance of me staying in Petakai to live out my days in blissful obscurity. Then, swinging open the captain's quarters, Alewic Azmi stepped out into the sunshine, beaming.

"Alewic?" Nalini asked with some volume, clearly surprised to see him on board. Alewic snapped his head towards us, immediately locking eyes with Nalini. Panic spread across his kind face, as confusion spread across mine and hers—though I doubted for the same reason. I realised quickly that Alewic's plans to return to Tabashi might not have been in the best interest of Petakai, and that maybe Petakai wasn't aware at all.

"Rimi!" the captain yelled.

Then I saw them, racing towards us on the harbour, a group of Petakai soldiers, calling for a scientist who had snuck onto a penjajap bound for a different kingdom. All of his brilliant discoveries, his life's work and designs, and how to use them, departing with him.

"Stop them!" they yelled, crashing into carts and stalls as they scattered across the docks. But we were off, flying with the swift wind that Rimi skillfully guided into our sails.

"What's happening here?" Nalini called out, but we lurched forwards; we had to grip onto the bannister to stop ourselves from falling. When I'd stabilised myself, I looked up to see the captain brandishing a sly grin stretching from ear to ear.

✹✹ 14 ✹✹

"Right, what's the meaning of this?" Nalini barked. We were all huddled in the captain's quarters. Nalini's sharp focus scanned the room, taking in each of our faces with suspicion. The air was musty with smells of old damp wood and piles of lontar. I had wrangled a dimple from Rimi just before we'd entered. It comforted me to know that her reasons for avoiding me were simply because of her anxieties about the departure, the secrecy of her father's escape. Now that we were safely on the seas, she had a reason to smile again, perhaps.

"First, I'd like to know why you're here on my penjajap, Nalini Singh," asked the captain from behind her desk, still brandishing her cocky grin from earlier. Nalini's steady gaze darted to the captain, her posture straightening as she prepared to answer. I leaned in too, eager to know what Petakai's council had decided for her, and for me.

"The council agreed that an alliance between Petakai and Tabashi would be fruitful for both our kingdoms. They've sent me as a gesture of good faith, and to present the offer," she replied steadily. I gritted my teeth in frustration. "Now you tell me why a royally commissioned scientist of Petakai is here on a ship—"

"Penjajap," the captain corrected.

"—bound for Tabashi without the proper authorities!" Nalini yelled.

"Nalini, please," Alewic started, his voice soft.

"Don't you dare, Ali," she snapped back. *Ali?*

"It's just titles, Nalini. You know why I can't stay," he replied, his tone reminding me of those shared between the crew of the *Bayanihan*. I realised they must have known each other long before their jobs demanded more from them than what they'd bargained for.

"Yes, but it's me who will have to answer for your crimes!" Nalini flared, her voice cracking. Silence gripped us. She breathed out all the air she held in her chest and fell into a cushioned chair. I finally saw how alone she was amongst all of us. Even I, having only just heard the whole truth myself, stood a ways away from Nalini—side by side with Alewic and Rimi and at the end of the room beside the captain. I realised then that you can have sympathy for the rich—if their experiences aren't so different from yours.

"Let's bring Petakai some good news then," I offered, and everyone turned to look at me with curiosity. Nalini—and by extension Petakai's council—had yet to personally reveal my part in their schemes. To them, my knowledge of the plans was inconsequential to their enactment. But I could only assume that whatever awaited me in Tabashi was now in Nalini's hands, so it couldn't hurt to extend mine.

"I give you a job, and a ship, and here you are with your schemes," Nalini said, looking back at the captain. We all let ourselves relax then. She was different outside of those marbled halls. Amongst peers, she held a strength of a different kind, a sureness of herself; she looked taller.

"Can't change me, Nalini," the captain said.

"They wanted my designs for their war," Alewic asserted.

"Alewic, there isn't an island on the map where you won't find someone after your weapons, and why are we talking about this in front of the Estari?"

"Her name is Linh," Rimi added sharply. I winced.

"*My* schemes," the captain teased.

"Her powers are unprecedented!" Nalini said as she rose from her chair to meet us. "I make every decision with no footing. No map. No guidelines. What would you have done?"

"That's right. What would you have done?" Alewic asked, standing his ground. We all had orders, the instructions we were told to follow, and all had our ways of betraying them; there was surely some truce to be found in that.

"How do you all know each other? If you don't mind me asking," I said finally. They all shared a look, earned from a time that was now long past.

"Nalini and I studied together at Vatthana," Alewic said. "That was when I met Rimi's mother." He reached an arm up to squeeze her shoulders.

"There are worse friends to have than the family who owns the place," joked the captain. A pang of anger, Rimi was thrown. Did her friends know that? Alewic bowed his head with humility and adjusted his robes. I wanted to tell him myself—but it wasn't my place.

"I met the captain before she was one," Nalini admitted.

"I was surrounded by highbrow academics trying to compose themselves on the high seas. Can you imagine that?" the captain said, and we all laughed. "Books don't prepare you for everything."

"They certainly do not," Alewic added, a little more solemnly.

"So what do we do this time around?" Nalini said, to change the mood that took us. "Firebombs? Or can we trust the Estari to save us?" She was familiar with the dangers then. I guessed she must have taken this passage before. *With the captain*, I thought, *or with a pirate?*

"We do what we've always done," the captain replied. "Survive."

"Linh?" Rimi asked.

It felt strange to still be addressed by that name after getting to know so many of them so well over those few days in Petakai. In a way, the stowaway had been right; I was using a dead girl's name, for we were all dead to the world, so what did it matter?

"I—I don't remember how... I'm not even sure what I did," I admitted. I heard exasperated sighs. I thought back to the fire, to that night, to the stowaway, the things that she showed me. Heat rushed to my face again, and I tried to bring my thoughts back into the room to calm myself down. Showing them what I'd learned about my magic meant explaining how I'd come about that knowledge, and I was not prepared to give them that just yet. I realised I was keeping the stowaway a secret, but it was one of the few chips I had left. Reader, I don't know if you've ever tried to play counting chips with a village girl, but if all she has is one chip, she will never lose a game.

"Well, Rimi, show the kid everything you know," the captain ordered, and I straightened my spine.

"Yes, Captain," Rimi said quickly and shot me a look of apprehension. The captain wasn't aware that I'd already asked the Azmis for help with my magic, and that they had none to give.

"We have three days to make the crossing," the captain continued, rising from her chair. "If we encounter the naga, it'll be on the third. Pray to Shi she doesn't find us before then."

* * *

I would never get used to, or grow tired of, the creaking of the wooden planks beneath my feet and the salty spray of the ocean on the wind. Each morning we would wake before the sun crept into the sky. Beginning the day with a cold breakfast in the galley before starting our chores. It took Nalini some time to get her own sea legs back, but I could tell that even she enjoyed the open air and the quiet comfort it brought her. I considered the story of a girl studying at an esteemed university meeting a pirate of the high seas. The adventures they would have had, only to eventually find themselves at the helm of a penjajap or at the seat of power in Petakai's council. I wondered if I would ever have such a spectacular tale of my own.

The sky above us was like a painting paired with the ocean below it, pillowing white clouds to match the churning foam of the waves. Rimi had gestured for me to follow her after our breakfast. We stood together on the deck, the tail of her braid flickered like a flame in the wind.

"When you saved me," she began, retrieving from her robes various materials that she then laid out on a barrel beside her, "you called a giant wave to push me back onto the *Bayanihan*. You called another wave to meet the naga."

"Powers of Shi," I mused.

"But it was strange—it wasn't an attack. It's like you spoke to it with the water," she revealed.

"How?" I asked.

"I don't know. That's just what I saw," she said. Then she retrieved a small silver round to hold up in front of me. "My father invented these. It's concentrated powder. When I hold them, I feel their potential. Normally I have to find the fire. I use half of my energy trying to get it started. With these, it's like the energy is right there waiting for me and all I have to do is let it out."

Rimi tossed a silver round into the air, then broke it with her magic. It crackled with a brilliant display of fluttering pink light. Then she handed me the pouch.

"I do not know if this will do anything for you, but we might as well try," she said.

"These are the same rounds as before, aren't they?" I asked.

"It was meant to be a distraction, for the naga and for you. I figured if you had something to keep your mind occupied, we wouldn't lose you to panic," she admitted, and I gulped. We were all just playing a game of counting with the chips we had in our deck.

"How do I do it again?" I asked playfully. But I knew how. Out of everyone there, Rimi deserved to know about the stowaway the most; she'd spent every day of the past week helping me. But I didn't know how to tell her, didn't know whose side either of them were on. Who

I'd be betraying. As I concentrated, I realised I couldn't do what Rimi had asked of me with the objects in my hand. The cool metal of the silver rounds, how dry it was. Working with them felt like trying to extract water from sand.

"This isn't working for me," I said apologetically and returned them to her.

"I thought as much. Here," she said, returning the silver rounds back into their pouch and retrieving a waterskin to place in my hands, "there's water in there."

I closed my eyes. It was hard—admittedly—with the entire ocean around us. Reader, I don't know if you've ever tried to spot a fish in the sea. If someone asked you to, and you'd never done it before, it can seem impossible. But if you wait for the light to catch it, you can sometimes see the flicker of its tail, a small silver sliver in the water. Then you might have a chance. So I waited. Letting myself grow familiar with the sounds of the sea, the depths of its breath. It began like a rumbling in my chest, a yearning to be set free. A door appeared, and I crept towards it. *Show me.*

Yanked out of the darkness by a force I couldn't see, I collapsed onto the deck. I was choking. Water rising from inside me and drowning me from the inside out—crashing into the walls of my mind, bursting through my vision, pouring out of my ears. But with my eyes open I realised that what I thought was happening to me was only in my mind, the sea a calm blanket buffered by the wind. Rimi was by my side in an instant.

"What happened?!" she asked.

"The water. It's everywhere," I sputtered, as if I was still drowning from the inside out, not sure what I meant myself. Looking up at her, I was grateful to behold a face full of understanding. On this whole penjajap, she was the only other person who could understand; what flowed from me to touch the tides flowed from her to tame the flame.

"My magic grew with me," she began, her arms outstretched and guiding me back to standing. "I've always known it. Another pair of eyes that I can never close. Eventually I got used to the brightness."

She helped to adjust my garments and brushed down the wrinkles, smiling gently as she said, "Take your time, Linh."

But time was a precious thing we didn't have, so I closed my eyes and tried again. I had felt it once. If it took bracing myself against a thousand floods, then so be it. *Show me*, I demanded with pursed lips, and threw open the door.

But that time it was different; I was ready, facing the torrent head-on. I felt all the ocean's rivers racing past to fill spaces all around me. Patiently waiting for the tides to settle so that I could find what I was looking for: my silver fish. Being surrounded by it on all sides, I soon noticed something moving against the grain: water that flowed upstream. I gasped. Standing right in front of me and spread out around the ship were people—bodies of water that collected like lakes on the land. It was breathtaking. I stayed there in the blue for as long as I could. All the different hues illuminated in my focus. A spectrum of how the water flowed to give us life or movement. When I finally found another pool, it was so small. Just a puddle, unlike the others. I concentrated on it, willed myself to remember it, eyes open. So when I attempted to pour a small amount of water out of the waterskin and onto the palm of my hand, an amount that I could control? Reader, it flew—a fish swimming upstream.

"Praise Shi!" Rimi exclaimed, and we both rejoiced.

"Well, it's a start," I said, but I couldn't deny my excitement. After a lifetime spent hiding this from everyone, myself included, it warmed me to no end to have it out there in the world—and for it to be celebrated.

15

For hours, we trained on the ship's deck. It wasn't easy, and I made many mistakes. I had to learn how to find the water quickly, to maintain my concentration on it even when all my other senses were distracting me. Focusing on the parts that I wanted to move from one place to another. I found it easier to pair my focus with the movements of my hands, similar to the ones Rimi made when she worked her magic on the sails. Outstretched in front of me to help guide the motion of the water through the air. It was all about focus. If my mind shifted, if I noticed the wind more than the tide, I lost it all. It was easier to find the currents with my eyes closed, but the edges were blurred without my other senses. I had to learn to see it all in the full light of day. I would practise this skill over the course of the morning. Eventually I could accumulate a greater amount and advance the complexity of its movements. Despite my nerves about the crossing, and the enormous task that awaited me should we meet the naga again, I was gaining a warm confidence—radiating out of my chest as the day wore on. I'd spent my whole life trying to find something I could be good at. Something to prove that I was more than a girl from nowhere with no title. I thought, *Finally. A chance.*

"Rimi," I began, in between our practice.

"Yes, Linh?"

I leaned in closer.

"What made you forgive the captain?" I asked quietly. The question had been playing on my mind all morning. Rimi sighed and looked around to see who was listening. Realising we were alone, she replied.

"That was the deal, why she let me on her ship. If they went down, her crew came first. I knew what I was signing up for."

"But you never intended for the ship to go down. She was going to follow through with it—"

"What's done is done," she said, too harshly. Maybe she hadn't yet fully forgiven the captain. Such is the consequence of choices made when there seemed to be no others.

"I appreciate your concern, truly, and I am so glad that you were there. But Tanh agreed to sneak my father onto the ship," Rimi admitted, turning to look at the captain standing silently at the helm. "She can't take back what she did, but she can make it up to me now."

I released the tension in my hands from trying to control the water.

"There are worse friends to have than the captain of the *Bayanihan*," Rimi said a little smugly. She had mimicked the captain's voice from earlier. It made me snicker.

"What are you two giggling about?" I heard from Alewic as he approached us.

"I caught a fish!" I lied quickly. Rimi and I locked eyes. Then we burst into riled cackling.

* * *

For a break from my training, the crew gave me simple tasks. Mostly, it was small things that they could trust me not to fail—or if I failed, it would not jeopardise the entire enterprise. Fishing was one of the more fun ones. Using nets and lines to catch fresh food for the day to be garnished with limes and chilli, then eaten raw. I practised spotting the fish in the ocean with my eyes open. Then I tried to find them in the currents with my eyes closed. It ended up being good practice for finding something small and moving against the grain.

Other times, the crew tasked me with cleaning. Less fun. I wished to use my magic to rid the wood of the damp, but I would notice Rimi warming herself by just throwing on another layer of robes, without the use of magic. Maybe every task shouldn't be solved with it. There was always an element of sacrifice, that part I understood. But we all weren't sure what the water would ask of me, so we had to play it safe—at least for now.

It felt good to be helping on the *Bayanihan*; we all relied on each other. If there was anything you couldn't do, or wanted to do but didn't know how, there was someone to ask and someone else to help. They had made the passage across the oceans many times, likely for years before Rimi ever boarded the ship—and I finally saw why; they had each other. There was nothing I wouldn't have done for my crew when I still had them.

As I went about my tasks, I approached one of them on the deck, a broad-shouldered man named Kato. He had warned me about having sea legs back in Tabashi. He had a stern look on his face, but his furrowed brow betrayed an age-worn kindness. "How long have you been with the *Bayanihan*?" I asked him.

"Since I was a boy," he said, rubbing his chin. His answer surprised me.

"But isn't the *Bayanihan* a new ship?"

"The penjajap is new, the *Bayanihan* is not. This crew is my family; we aren't bound by a vessel. I've only ever known the open seas, can't imagine what you would want on dry lands, especially ones as dry as Tabashi," he said, then collected himself to apologise.

"It's alright. I have no reason to defend it," I said plainly. He queried me with his gaze.

"So why return?"

"I have no choice," I admitted.

"There's always a choice," he said with a serious face. Was he just like the captain? I wondered if he had known her when she was still a pirate, how long ago that could have been. We were quickly approached by a petite woman named Yuna. I had spoken to her before too—on my first day on the *Bayanihan*. She was always quick to joke and was proud of her busy hands on the ship. "What about you, Yuna?" he asked her as she nudged him. "Thoughts on Tabashi?"

"They make the best rice wine," she said gleefully.

"A lot of us are out here on the sea because we prefer it," Kato said thoughtfully.

"No politics out here, or at least none you can't settle with your machete," Yuna added.

"Whose side are you on?" Kato addressed me evenly.

"Side?" I repeated. "Do you mean between Tabashi or Petakai?"

"No, you're a Tabashi girl, right? Haven't you seen the protests?" he pressed. I realised he was talking about the writing I'd seen on the docks, of the letters in red.

"I try to stay out of it," I said quickly. If the seas were so borderless, why was Kato interested in Tabashi's politics? Was he also testing me?

"You look different," Yuna said to me. "Expensive."

"It's not something I'm used to," I assured her.

"Oh, we know," she said confidently. "We've been taking bets on where you're really from."

"Yuna," Kato hissed under his breath. I felt a storm rolling in my chest.

"What? We've got to find out if someone's going to win," she smirked, and they both laughed. I felt suddenly unsteady and held myself up against the balustrade. I wondered if now, far from being just another crew member, I was their cargo to protect.

"Have you always been an Estari?" she asked, her face lighting up. "I've a cousin who can control the sails like the Exorci does, wild thing."

"Her name is Rimisin," I said coldly and left them to their tasks.

"What did I say?" I heard in hushed tones behind me as I made my way over to the other side of the ship. There was no real way to find privacy on the penjajap. All of our sleeping quarters were shared except for the captain's. It was then that I spotted her leaning against the balustrade, face to the sun.

"Captain," I addressed her evenly as I found a spot beside her.

"Yes?" she said, barely raising an eyebrow.

"Do you trust your crew?" I asked boldly. I wasn't sure what had come over me. The girl who was once too afraid to ask too many questions was somehow ready to start a mutiny.

"With my life, and me with theirs," she replied without pause. "Is something wrong?"

I sighed and rested the weight of my body on my forearms, leaning over the ocean and looking out to the distant horizon.

"You think you have a handle on things, that you know what's going on, and then everything changes. Now you're in brand-new clothes on your way back to the place you were running from."

"Running?" she repeated, finally turning to face me. I didn't respond. She caught sight of the two that I'd been speaking to from across the deck; they were still gossiping.

"At least look busy!" she called out to them, masking a chuckle. "Did they tell you about the bet?"

"I hope one day I can be talked to and not about," I retorted. She placed a steadying hand on my back.

"They actually mean well. Consider it an initiation. You saved us, kid; remember that."

"That's the problem; I can't. Every time I try to recall that night, my mind goes blank."

"I see."

"What if I can't do it again? What if I've doomed us?"

"Already doomed," she mused. I wanted to ask her about Nalini, and also about Rimi. Wanted to ask what she really thought of Exorci. The captain and the crew were treating us differently. I felt that it was unfair. Rimi had chosen—fought for a place—to be on the ship so she could make it safer, yet her magic filled them with doubt. I had merely stumbled upon the power that saved them. It was a coincidence that I was there at the right time to do so. I had boarded the *Bayanihan* to abandon it. Me, trusted in all my lies. Rimi, feared in the face of her truths.

"It's much simpler out here," I heard the captain say next to me as if answering my thoughts. "No laws, no council. You've just got to figure out the next bite to eat and where to go to get it."

"How did you and Nalini meet?" I asked. They seemed oceans apart, and yet there was no denying what was between them. I caught the sly smile that curled the captain's lips.

"She found me in a tough spot and got me out of it."

"I can't help but feel like she's put me in one," I challenged.

"The alliance between Petakai and Tabashi has been fraught for decades," the captain revealed, and I thought back to the tension in the council meetings. Despite Nalini's position of leadership, Petakai's council had to operate as a united front—and their foundations were crumbling. "Nalini's fighting for peace."

"Then why is she so hard on me?" I pressed.

"She knows you're lying," she replied darkly. I swallowed my words and readied myself to retrieve the dagger strapped to my waist, though I had no idea what I'd do with it. "Nalini can read people like a book. I think it's her beauty that disarms them," the captain said, smiling and turning to face me. "It's alright; you can keep your secrets. Shi knows we've all got them."

With that, she turned to leave me, her final words called out over her shoulder. "I'll keep Nalini off your back," she said with a smirk and a sly twinkle in her eye.

* * *

As the sun began its slow descent into the sea, I made my way below deck towards the ship's stock. We had no open flames on the ship, a fire was dangerous, and the crew believed the heat would attract the naga. So once it got too dark to see, we would gather to sleep in our shared quarters. Our bellies full from cold meals prepared in the day's light as it trickled in from glass prisms built into the deck. If you caught it at the right time, you could admire an entire spectrum of colour reflected onto the interior wood of the hull.

My spirits were high and my breaths were steady. I'd told myself that I had just wanted to double-check my numbers, but as the darkness of the cargo hold met me, I realised what I was doing. I stopped myself on the bottom step, turned, and raced back up to the light. Just as I was about to make my way to our sleeping quarters, I noticed two shadows moving about in the captain's quarters.

"Cowards," I heard Nalini hiss.

"Well, you're not wrong," replied the captain.

"They want the ship to go down. They're trying to get rid of me. You can see that, right?"

"Of course."

"They'll never let me have this. Every room I've been in, I've had to kick down the door just for them to try and throw me out."

"Probably because you kicked down their door."

"And you're no help."

"What did I do?"

"You're always looking at me. They know. They must know."

"I can't help it. You're always worth looking at."

I heard a thump. Something heavy on the table. I decided it was best to leave them be. They must have had a lot of catching up to do. I hastily made my escape and ran right into Rimi.

"Linh, good evening," Rimi greeted me with a courteous smile.

"Rimi! Just the person I was looking for," I blurted. She raised her eyebrow. "I—I thought maybe we could try to find a way around the naga."

"What?" she replied, echoing the words in my head; I was improvising in my panic.

"Between you and me, I'm sure there's something we could find that the others can't read—something that might give us an advantage as we sail." The words spilled out of me as quickly as I could invent them, but then I realised I might be on to something. Rimi must have felt the same, because she slowly nodded in agreement and followed me away from the captain's quarters and into the navigation room. I knew we could find some maps of the waters there, and possibly trace a new journey through them with what we could read about the currents using our magic.

We entered to find Alewic—with his own drawings sprawled out across the table.

"Oh! Hello—" Alewic said.

"Linh thinks we can avoid the naga altogether," Rimi answered to his surprise.

"Maybe, but I can't figure it out alone. Would you like to help?" I confessed to Alewic. He nodded, rolling up his drawing and unfurling maps of the sea. Rimi came and stood by my side. Her finger traced the same currents I was examining, and Alewic leaned in to follow us. When I shut my eyes, I could feel the warmth of the water, and I knew there was something to be made of that. "The currents flow this way, bringing in warmer water from the south," I suggested, outlining the path with my finger.

Alewic's face lit up with curiosity. "How do you know that?" he asked.

"I can just feel it," I admitted.

"Me too," Rimi added, sustaining my confidence. "Linh is right."

Alewic turned over a new idea forming in his mind. "Snakes can see us at night because they detect the heat of our bodies," he said. "There's no way of knowing what the naga sees, but if its anatomy is anything to go by, that could be our answer."

"We already know they're attracted to the fire," Rimi added, her eyes sharpening to a point. "The naga finds the barrels almost immediately once I set them alight."

"Even if the naga is finding us by detecting the heat on our ship," I said, "perhaps we can find the right current, warm enough that the heat from our bodies gets mixed in with the surrounding current, confusing the creature," I added, my excitement growing. "I don't know if the naga sees the currents the way that I do—but if it does, we might just sneak past."

The room was silent. I had to look up to confirm whether they had heard me, but as soon as I saw their faces, it was obvious they had. We all wore the expression of children who had just uncovered a secret that the grownups wouldn't want us to know. It was late, so we took those secrets with us past dinner and into our hammocks for the evening, ready to discuss our plans with the captain come sunrise. Lying in my hammock below deck, swaying with the tides, my mind swirled with the day's conversations and the growing control I had on my powers. For the first time, I could imagine new possibilities—a path before me that wasn't about running or hiding. There were things that I could discover and ways that I could be helpful to those around me. Hearing the deep snores and steady breaths of the crew—the people whose faces and laughter I had grown used to—I felt much less afraid of the dark. *I could get used to this.*

But, inevitably, the solemn tinge of a familiar loneliness crept in. *Not now,* I thought. I had almost spent an entire day without it. *Let me have this.* And I squeezed my eyes shut to welcome the darkness that enveloped me. Willing sleep to race to find me before the memories did. That night, for the first time in a long time, sleep won.

* * *

In the morning, I sprang up from the greatest rest I'd had in decades. I raced past the crew, gathering themselves for breakfast, and almost sailed straight into the door to the captain's quarters. Stopping just before with breathless excitement, rapping on the door with the same force of my body's weight against the soles of my feet. If it didn't open soon I feared I might just topple over.

"It's too early for this!" yelled the captain from behind the door, and I chuckled in response.

"Too early to suggest how we avoid the naga?" I teased at the large wooden door. It opened quickly—but not all the way. The captain stood blocking the view inside her quarters with her body by the door. With bed sheets loosely clutched to her bare chest, I could tell that I'd interrupted something . . . important.

"Come back after breakfast," she commanded in a groggy voice. She was interested in listening to our proposal but was much too preoccupied at the time. I returned to the galley for a light breakfast of smoked meats washed down with a cracked-open coconut and the refreshing water found within. The captain joined us soon after, followed by Nalini. They both had a noticeable perk to their steps, and we all enjoyed the friendly cheer they brought to the meal. The conversations we shared carried me to another time when I had planned to make this journey for a very different reason, and with very different company. We had made many plans, admittedly. Ways to run away together and make a name for ourselves. The brilliant schemes that only young minds can conjure, because they don't know how easily ideas are blown away by a harsh wind. Perhaps that's why I watched the captain with Nalini so intently; there was something there that they had that I was still waiting for.

After breakfast, I returned with Alewic, Nalini, and Rimi to the captain's quarters to further discuss our plans. The captain had agreed to try them as we sailed closer to Tabashi's shores. We were all huddled in that room in a familiar scene, but this time we were all on the same side.

"Linh, you may have made this passage even safer for years to come," Alewic said, resting a gentle hand on my shoulder and squeezing it encouragingly. "Exorci will be essential on the ships now to read the currents just like you did last night." Rimi was beaming, and Alewic joined in on my training that day—excitedly expressing his delight at my growing capabilities. He made a festivity out of every success and offered comforting solace with every spill. Sharing stories of when Rimi was still learning to practise her own magic. I watched the memories touch both of their hearts.

"I feel closer to her out here," Rimi admitted about her mother—after I'd successfully raised a small orb of water out of the sea and sent it back down. That was the first time I'd heard her talk about it of her own volition, the first sign that she trusted me enough. It had meant a great deal to me, but the lightness of my gratitude was soon weighed down by the heft of shame. I was burdened by betrayal; Rimisin Azmi still did not know my real name.

"Is that why you still cross the ocean? To be close to her?" I asked her carefully.

"And to make sure no other child has to grow up without a mother," she replied soberly. But Rimi's thoughtful words had hit me like a tidal wave. The swell caught in my throat, and the wind was again knocked out of my sails. The ship that had been so carefully and so gently steered into calmer seas was suddenly swept away in the torrent. I quietly retreated into myself after that conversation, focusing on my magic and the steady raising and lowering of the tide. It wasn't Rimi's fault. How could she have known? It wasn't something we'd ever talked about. Guilt eventually calmed the cyclone that swirled. Rimi had memories that she shared with another, half a lifetime that was cut off too soon. She had a reason and a face for her grief. How could I mourn the loss of something I've never had?

Linh Tabashi. It meant that we belonged to the city. That we were found alone and given to its care. It's why all the children at the Eyrell were so difficult to control, and why no one looked for us when we all disappeared after the fire—*the ones with no title.*

✳✳ 16 ✳✳

The Eyrell was one of the few schools in the kingdom, built farthest out from the city and along its dangerous border. The Council had built all the schools, but the Eyrell relied solely on donations from the neighbouring villagers. We were the roughest and the loudest, because we had no one waiting for us to come home. Though it wasn't yet a common practice to send every child to school, with some villagers still preferring to teach their young by old ways of story and song, there had to be a place to send the unkept ones, to keep them from wandering into more trouble.

Our teachers tried to tell us we were lucky in that way. But we all knew that the village elders held wisdom that grounded them to the land as deep as the roots of the oldest trees in the Jungle, and that there was nothing more worthwhile than your understanding of that ancestry and your place in it all. It's why the children who had only ever grown up in the city could end up so lost, adrift on the breeze and at the mercy of its calling. But I had someone waiting for me to come home; I had a best friend. She would come looking for me as the days wore on, wouldn't ever let me wander too far out without a tether to pull me back again. It's no wonder that I was lost in the years that followed, maddened by the breeze. Even if it had been my ancestors calling, I wouldn't have known their voices and I wouldn't have recognised them if I'd tried; hers was the only one I listened out for.

* * *

The heat of the long days beat down on our skin, marked by the salt in the air and the relief of the cool breeze on our sun-scorched faces as it rose ever higher in the sky without a tree or cloud to cover it. But at least the sky was clear of storms, and the ship rocked gently—waves lapping at its sides. We were always on the watch for a shadow in the water too large to mistake for any other.

The crew, with their constant laughter and support, reminded me of how the children of the Eyrell would band together in times of need, conspiring to steal sticky rice. I felt I could trust them because I knew what mattered to them, that they ultimately only mattered to each other. I didn't have mine, but I could appreciate theirs; I knew what it meant, and I was grateful for their steady presence and the humour they shared. I knew I would miss it when I eventually would have to leave the ship and all those moments behind. But I pushed those thoughts aside and focused on the task at hand. Rimi would call on the wind with her powers to steady us whenever there was a hint of bad weather on the horizon. The precision in her movements, the confidence in her control—how long had it taken her to master her manipulation of the heat? What did she see in the starless sky? I asked her once how she did it, what she was whispering when she worked. Her magic was something she had always possessed, and its use came to her like air to breathe, or words to speak.

"Intention, practice, faith. It's a meditation," she said, arms raised to the sky. "I can move the heat much easier than I can start a fire; it's why my dad's powders are so valuable to us."

I looked back down towards the *Bayanihan*, at the people who maintained it. Everyone's life was made easier because of the designs of brilliant minds like Alewic, the compassion of hearts like Rimi's, and the difficult negotiations of leaders like Nalini and the captain. What did it take to become someone like that, where people's lives were better for them existing in it? As my return to Tabashi loomed, I couldn't shake the thought that I was sailing into a trap. The memories of the oppressive heat, the barren streets, and the constant hunger were all still so fresh in my mind from when we'd left the shore. Would I ever be able to escape the hardship that had been my life before joining the *Bayanihan*, before embarking on this journey towards a new one?

There on the ship was a chance to make something of myself—to prove that I was more than just a girl from nowhere with no title. I tried calling the tides to help Rimi with propelling the ship forward with speed. I couldn't imagine the toll that her efforts took on her body. There she was every day, diligent and masterful with the sails, and she never complained, despite the crew that barely trusted her. But Rimi had also warned me about doing too much with my own powers. She wanted nothing more from my magic until we reached Tabashi, unless it was absolutely necessary. She did not know how to guide me further into its use and feared my powers were far too great or too dangerous to let loose. *What if you capsized the ship? Caused a tsunami? Caused harm to yourself?*

"You need your strength, Linh. It's the part of my magic that I haven't quite figured out yet. But nothing is for free. When you fought the naga that night, you were out for three whole days."

"But I want to help," I pleaded. Despite everything that I was doing to become stronger and more capable, I still felt so out of control and with so little sway in the things that mattered.

"We can't lose you. What we've been practising . . . it's the small stuff."

"And so I'll never be ready."

"If we're lucky, and your navigation plans work, then you won't have to be."

Realising that there was no more to be discussed on the topic, I busied myself with a usual occupation. I checked that no one would follow me as I made my way below deck. Accepting that it was a habit that I had picked up and now couldn't shake. I was just checking the records. That's all it was, or at least that's what I told myself it was. But I knew that deep down, I was hoping she was there. Hiding out behind the barrels. I couldn't imagine how—but she'd done it the first time, and possibly many more times before then. I had almost given up—but then I heard it, a step I didn't place. My heart leapt into my throat.

"How has nobody found you yet?" I asked quietly, fighting the quiver in my voice. The excitement beat through my chest.

"You're the only one who comes down here, so you tell me," she replied, emerging from the shadows and making her way over to me. "Why has nobody come looking for me?" she asked, and our bodies were so close that I could feel the heat radiating off of her. I had to step back to stop myself from evaporating completely. "You like me," she teased.

"I don't trust you," I countered. She let out a low chuckle.

"Both can be true," she said, before walking away again. It couldn't have been easy for her, hiding out down there as the days wore on. She must have made her way above deck once the night took us all to bed. I had so many questions. What was she eating? Where did she sleep? Even ridiculous ones: how did she relieve herself? It must have been incredibly lonely.

"What's your story?" I called after her.

"Same as anyone's," she replied, turning back to face me. "Struggle. Hardship. Protecting the people I love."

"By stealing?"

"If I have to," she said, holding up the palm leaves I'd written on with the falsified records. "So what's your excuse?"

"What?" I said defensively.

"Perjury. Fraud," she continued, trying to contain a smirk. "You're quick to judge for someone on the run. Who are you running from?"

"Would you believe me if I said I didn't know?" I asked her, thinking I'd said something very clever—wondering how she disarmed me so easily. Wondering if it was for the same reason that the captain could for Nalini. She looked at me, her gaze softening.

"I would," she replied. We stood there on the solid planks, letting the gentle rocking of the tides guide us.

"Do you have any idea what's going to happen when we get back?" I asked, feeling a hint of fear creep in, hoping she could be the one to tell me the truth.

"I know what I have to do," she answered steadily.

"I'm going to be taken to the city," I said in defence—though I'm not sure who was attacking. "They're going to make me their symbol, aren't they? For the Prophecy?"

I assumed the stowaway was from Tabashi, that she would know what I was talking about without me having to explain it. We were all brought up with myths and legends of old—lessons paid for by the Council. All of Tabashi's citizens knew of the Prophecy: that a new age would reign once the rightful heir returned to the kingdom, and that it was the Council who held onto the throne until they did. I was always too busy playing with my best friend to listen. How those lessons seemed to truly matter now. But the stowaway didn't respond, and I couldn't help but feel a pang of loneliness in the memories that weren't shared.

"Do you have any business in the palace? Will you be there?" I asked, searching.

"Do you want me to be?" she teased; her words felt like they were poised at the tip of her machete. I felt a scalding heat burn from my nape and I quickly turned away. But then I heard Linh's name being called from above deck. I had to get back quickly before they came looking.

"Don't miss me too much," she called out after me, her voice full of smoke.

* * *

As night fell, we would gather in the galley to share a rehydrated serving of rice and vegetables. Not wanting to risk the unnecessary use of heat to cook, the meal would be prepared on land and then left out to bake in the sun.

The dried remains could be kept on the ship and brought back with some clean water and a lot of patience; it wasn't amazing, but after a long busy day on the ship it was more than enough. We would eat this cold dish with dried fruit for dessert, before it got too dark to see, and then retire to our beds to sleep the night away. It was cramped and dark below deck, but there was always a way to warm our spirits without a fire. We brightened the night with songs of our villages and full-hearted laughter—a sound I had missed dearly. A few of the crew would always have an instrument with them. Yuna would pull out a well-worn khlui, a simple bamboo flute perfect for slipping into one's pockets. Kato had made a makeshift version of a flat-bottomed lute, stringed with dried guts—we would call a phin. Paired with a ching, small domed finger cymbals joined with a cord that ran through the middle of them, the spontaneous band would play. The rest of us would dance and sing. We had few belongings on the ship, just enough to get us through the journey, but the people of these lands and seas would never go without music.

I welcomed the merriment and felt our spirits rise like the flames of a raging campfire burning against the burdening dark. Though I wasn't ever one for sunsets before, for the creeping of the purple night and the dreams it came with, there was no better way to spend the coming of it than with a meal amongst familiars and some music to tune our thoughts. Letting my mind travel with the guiding voices of the singers, memories would come in and out of view like a sinking sun through the clouds. It was always easier to face them surrounded by warm smiles and arms topping up a cup of rice wine. In between songs, I shared the story of how I nearly got swindled into turning over my coin for a useless trinket back at the markets on Tabashi's shores. That story felt like it was a world away to me then. Joking about how the merchant had claimed the trinket was from Petakai and a relic of Moultisjka the Terrible.

"Moultisjka, you say? Well, say it enough times and it becomes real," Alewic countered as we all ate our meal. "That name has become so much more about what it means to different people than the woman who once held it." I heard murmurs of agreement from the crew.

"Some believe that she really is still alive," said Kato, "that she's the leader of the Bashantu."

"The Bashantu?" I repeated, curious. I had heard that name before, serving pints in the taverns, catching bits of gossip as I spilled yet another round of drinks on the floor before I could get to serving them, mopping them up with rags.

"Bandits," replied Rimi, without missing a beat. I searched for the meaning behind her tone.

"Mercenaries, more like. They're no small group," Alewic countered.

"So what's their motive?" I asked pointedly.

"Your guess is as good as ours. They steal goods. From the docks or city markets," replied the crew member. Red flashed across my mind. Threats that were thrown out at the end of a blade. Numbers I had to explain. The warmth of a hand in mine. *The stowaway?*

"You'd better hope they haven't heard about your powers by the time we reach port. It's a long journey to the palace, and I'd wager they'd love a bargaining chip like the saviour of Tabashi," Rimi teased, finishing her bowl.

"What do you mean by that?" I said too harshly.

"The Prophecy," she appealed, surprised by my tone. So she knew; they all knew. I felt bile rising in my throat that made it difficult to swallow any more of my meal. I looked around at the faces of the crew. How much of the Prophecy did they all believe? Were we all just waiting for a saviour to return to change things? That's what the stowaway had meant, whose side she was really on. A Bashantu. Despite my company continuing on with the conversation, I remained silent, realising that some things were better left unspoken. Eventually, when I found the courage to excuse myself, I handed the rest of my meal to Kato; he gobbled it.

"Tired already?" Rimi asked me with a worried expression. I tried to reassure her she was right, not wanting to draw any more attention to myself, and swiftly made my way back to my hammock. But as I tried to lie down and tuck myself in, the storm surged. The rage in my chest was unshakable. How could I have been so foolish? How could I have been so callous, so quick to trust? I tossed and turned in my hammock. I'd revealed to the Bashantu the full extent of my powers. No wonder she was helping me to hone them; I was a tool for their cause, just as I had been to Petakai.

I soon found the stream where I had first heard about the Bashantu. It was during a private conversation amongst peers, similar to the one we'd just shared at dinner. At the back of a tavern. Hushed because she spoke of the rebellion. A mounting tension amongst the people to bring total power into question. To challenge the Prophecy and the Council that gave themselves the throne in place of a lost royal lineage. I was piecing together the parts of the story that were being withheld from me; Tabashi's council were waiting for a rightful heir, Petakai's were waiting for them to pay off their debts, the Bashantu were waiting for a symbol for their uprising. That's what my powers had meant to all of them: a spark to kindling for the wildest fire our kingdoms had ever seen. It didn't matter if any of it was true or not. Just like it didn't matter if the children being taken from their homes had any powers. There was enough fear being governed in the maintenance of an elaborate lie, and I could finally see the threads woven into the tapestry of Tabashi's.

The curse of searching for a missing girl I'd known too long ago had plagued me into blind naivety; it had to end. I couldn't keep being at the mercy of the pull of strings tied by hands that I couldn't hold to steady them. What other secrets, what other dangers awaited me as I returned to the place that I'd spent the past week running from? I shot up in my hammock. My mind raced, feeling blood collecting in my throat. I had to tell the captain. I had to tell *somebody*. But another thought stopped me: if this had always been the stowaway's plan—the Bashantu's—and if she realised I knew, that I'd figured it out, then surely she would try anything to stop me from revealing her secrets. The best time for a body to go missing is late at night beneath the tide. I didn't know whose lives I'd be risking with the truth.

Rimi had given me that small blade back at port, a beautiful but deadly thing. I had thought it queer; the only other people she knew I had to look out for were the crew on the ship and the captain. In all our meetings, it was the captain who had come to my defence, who had fought for my freedoms. But the captain trusted her crew, and it was to the crew she answered. She'd so easily sacrifice an Exorci to spare their lives. *A pirate*, I reminded myself—*for a price on my head*. I realised how alone I was on the ship. Rimi and her father were the only people I could trust—two people also on the run, also at the mercy of the way the currents took them. I gripped the handle of the blade hard and held it to my chest, taking in as many breaths as I needed to steady my racing heart.

That night I rallied a recurring race against the spreading claws of restless sleep. That night, regrettably, my memories won.

✳︎✳︎ 17 ✳︎✳︎

Less than a day from port, I felt a familiar thunderous quiet as it reverberated across the ship. We all treaded lighter that day, minding our steps, keeping our voices low. The captain had steered us steadily, working with Rimi on the sails. I had thought to tell her in the morning about the fears I had—my theories about the captain, and the truth about the stowaway, but I reminded myself of the risk. If I revealed to Rimi that there might be a Bashantu on the ship, what then? So close to port. What could be done about it now? I decided I would tell them everything I knew once we reached port—once we were safely on land. But Rimi could tell that something was wrong with me that day. She'd tried many times to reassure me that we would make it safely back to Tabashi's shores—thinking that must be why I was so nervous. I took her reassurance willingly; I didn't want to worry her further. She must already have had so much to think about—her father on the ship, sailing across the same ocean where she had lost her mother. I would have to deal with my worries alone.

During the morning, I wandered back down towards our sleeping quarters to pack up my belongings, to make sure that I wouldn't leave anything behind. But I heard hushed voices in the hull, and I lay myself flat against the wall outside to listen.

"What do you think will happen?" I heard from Kato.

"I don't know. But the Exorci bring death," responded Yuna, her voice and disdain so distinct. "It doesn't matter who they appear to be; it's Moultisjka's magic in their veins."

"And what of the Estari? The Prophecy?"

"Anamashta's heir? You believe that?"

"Doesn't matter what we believe if the Council buys it."

"And what of the people? The rebellion? Will they buy it?"

"Who's to say."

I crept away from the door and back up towards the deck, my mind churning with what I'd just overheard. Even Kato and Yuna were discussing my part in the grand schemes of others, and I wanted nothing more to do with it all. I had only just learned about my own powers, and now I was caught in the swell of something much larger than myself. Suddenly, out of the corner of my eyes, two young girls raced to catch each other from across a field of dry rice stalks, laughing with irrational delight as they ran down the length of the bannister of the ship. My pace quickened; I ran to keep up with them.

"You'll never catch me, Moultisjka!" one of them called out to the other.

"Get back here, Anamashta, and finish what you started!" she called out to me. We were just playing pretend, brandishing those names as if they could take us out of our world and into one where magic was real and we had a fighting chance. I watched the girls leap off the edge of the *Bayanihan* and into the water. I threw myself against the balustrade, arms reaching down into the sea. But there was nothing there. Only the steady rocking of the blue breaking against itself. It wasn't real; it couldn't have been. My body forced me to take in a breath before I choked without one.

I looked back at the crew and caught wind of all the other currents swirling about above deck that day: the schemes of others, their greed for wealth or power or even for . . . love? A look shared between the captain and Nalini—perhaps it was simply all for her, and to that I felt myself soften. There was nothing I could do with my assumptions; I didn't have the full picture, couldn't grasp the inner workings of their minds or know their stories. Who knew the ways the world worked against them? Whose favour they were pining for. I resigned myself to the shadow of things unknown—a familiar darkness. The captain, this ship, and its loyal crew had granted me safe passage across the seas—and I safety from the naga in return; it was a fair deal. It was time for my plans to be put to the test. I closed my eyes to feel the currents beneath us, felt the way the heat of the water in our bodies blended with the waters all around us, willed the edges to blur further, to keep us hidden—not knowing if that was even possible or within my power. Finding Rimi sitting at the edge of the ship, her gaze trained on the horizon, I approached her quietly—not wanting to startle her.

"Rimi," I whispered. "I need to talk to you."

"Off the starboard bow," we heard from above, as quietly as their voice could allow. We all turned to see the looming dark figure in the water, still some ways away—seemingly undisturbed by our presence. I gripped the bannister. It would have to wait. The shadow ahead, larger than any ship could create, swished and swirled in the distance.

"Easy does it," the captain called out to Rimi, who had softened her pull on the wind. Our speed waned. We drifted slowly in the shadow's way. All our breaths held. A deafening silence billowing on the inside of my head till all I could hear was the thumping of my beating heart. It moved towards us, the shadow. Ever so slowly. An ink spill suspended in the deep. Some members of the crew reached for their weapons, hands firmly wrapping around the grip of their machetes.

"Easy," warned the captain.

I watched as the looming terror snaked under our ship. If I hadn't been so terrified, I might have marvelled at its beauty beneath the waves, the way its scales shimmered, catching the afternoon light. After what felt like an eternity, its long body trailing endlessly behind it, we saw the unmistakable swish of the end of its tail sink below—and then past—the stern of the ship. I turned to Rimi. Her eyes were wide and wild. I realised I had a pair to match. But then she welcomed a tentative and hopeful smile. I mirrored that too. It was too soon to celebrate, but I could feel the tension subsiding in the crew with a collective exhale. The captain, hands still steady on the wheel, signed to Rimi to bring back the wind. Rimi raised her right hand, swirling it into a fist. The sails bellowed. We all silently cheered. I made my way back towards the stern and peered out over the water to catch a final glimpse of the naga. My body reacted before my mind could.

Two eyes beneath the tide, twin moons of sacred blue flame, were staring right back at me from the deep. The snaking body of the naga curling underneath it like the sign I had seen in the harbour. Without thinking, I bowed my head, a known sign of respect in our kingdom, of thanks and of humility. I raised my head back up in time to see the image in the water slowly fade with the rippling of the waves. *Thank you*, I whispered in my heart and sent it across the channel. I didn't know why at the time—it had just felt instinctual to do so.

There were parts of the story that we were told as kids that we wouldn't listen to because it was never as fun as the battles; it was the parts about their demise. About what happens after we die, where we go—or rather, where Shi takes us. Sometimes, if our spirits have a reason to linger, we find ourselves back here again, in the closed system, back in the bodies of the beings and the beasts that we wronged. So our souls could know their pain, and one day, in another life, come to their salvation. Perhaps every soul still trapped here owed it to each other to find a way out again. I think wherever we are going, we can only go together. Otherwise, why are we all still trapped?

* * *

Rising out of the blue horizon were the climbing peaks and spires of the beautiful stone-white city, reaching up into a clear burning sky. The kingdom of Tabashi expanded out to meet us, and we were finally close enough that I could make out its distinct features—so different from Petakai's city. The thatched-roof huts and houses on stilts, and further up the valley, whitewashed buildings surrounded by a dry field that from that distance took on a yellow hue in the sunlight—a golden sea stretched out from the shores.

A part of me ached. It's not that I didn't want to call it home—the beautiful land, the sea of rice. But in that place, I'd had so much taken from me, the memories so vivid every time I breathed in the arid air; it was like being constantly choked by the fire. Though I was returning with a new purpose, in a new set of clothes, and even about to don a new name, I hoped that over time I could make some memories strong enough to erase the hurt of the old.

As the ship approached the harbour, I felt the excitement from the crew; their smile lines deepened with the approaching coast. After three long days at sea, the sight of land was a welcome relief. We all looked forward to hot meals, solid ground, and a much-needed break from the constant sway of the ship on the water. So we prepared to dock; the crew moved about with a new sense of urgency, executing their orders with practised precision and control, quickly tying up the ropes and lowering the sails. The *Bayanihan* rocked one final time as it settled in beside the jetty.

"Praise Shi!" the captain cried out, and a loud cheer erupted from us all. It was a boisterous cry, filled with relief that we all had been saving for the shore. A buffalo horn blared from the harbour, adding to the celebration, and I turned my attention to the gathering crowd on the docks. People of all ages were clapping and cheering, welcoming us back to Tabashi. The *Bayanihan* had safely landed, and the joy on the faces of the people who had accumulated to see its return was indescribable. The crew gathered by the balustrade and waved to what I could only assume were their families and loved ones. It hadn't occurred to me they still had people waiting for them back on land—but of course they did; most people had someone waiting for them to come home.

I turned to say my goodbyes as Kato hoisted me up into a weighty embrace. Yuna followed close behind and did the same, though she couldn't lift me up quite as high.

"Don't be a stranger," she said to me, grinning—and I returned it absolutely; they were just following orders—doing the best they could with the information they had. They feared the things they were taught to fear. How could I blame them for the stories we had all been brought up with? I vowed, above anything else, that if I had a chance to make things right, I would. People had to know of the good of the Exorci, of the battles they fought to help us survive—despite the darkness that shrouded them. Then the captain appeared to give me a stiff clap to the shoulders.

"Until we meet again. It's been a pleasure, kid," she said.

"Likewise, Captain. Thank you," I replied earnestly.

"No, thank you. You do not know the lives you've saved today—and all days," she said, bowing her head. "Call me Tanh," she added with a wink. "You made it this far. You've earned it."

"Where will you go next?" I asked quickly. "And what of the stock?"

"It's headed into the markets. I should go with it to make sure nothing goes missing," she replied, and I felt the snaking vines of guilt slither up behind me and constrict around my throat. I thought to tell her, spurred on by my struggle for air, thinking, *Now or never*, but then caught sight of Nalini crossing the deck with her luggage in tow, only to hand it off to what I could only assume would be her chaperone through the kingdom. Nalini shared a look with Tanh, then politely nodded to Captain Tanhchana Wardhani of the *Bayanihan*, as she was Nalini Singh of the council of Petakai. It made my chest ache. Again, now was not the time.

Reader, I'd rather have choked to death than ruin a moment between them.

But then the captain made a subtle gesture with her hands by her side. It was only slight, and I caught the twinkle in Nalini's eyes in response to it. It was the same wordless communication they'd used that day in the council meeting, of that I had no doubt. They'd found a way to communicate across borders and policies so that the things that mattered could always be said.

"Now, where can I get some fresh sticky rice?" I heard Alewic say as he wrapped his arms around our shoulders and squeezed them, inspiring a chuckle. It temporarily knocked the vines loose, and I breathed in the jovial air. The captain turned back to me and bowed her head again before taking her leave. I wished to say more to her, but I did not know what. It was such a quick goodbye for what had felt like an entire lifetime together. But there was nothing else to it, so we headed off the ship.

TAPESTRIES OF A KINGDOM

* * *

As Rimi, Nalini, and I navigated through the bustling crowd, we assisted Alewic with his hastily gathered luggage from Petakai. Nalini conversed with the guards on the docks until they handed us over to the escort of a company of palace guards—shirtless soldiers with circlets of gold and chains that hung across them attached to their sheathed swords, their sompot chong kben in a material likened to the scales of vipers, rippling in the light; some guards preferred to wrap their chests with a plain cotton garment beneath their chain link. In the past, I would nervously peer out the window of the Eyrell at the guards that marched through the streets, parading a line of new Exorci soldiers, their faces hidden by their cloaks. There were often parades of power and boasts of the wealth and mercy of the Council through these lands; they grew more common with each passing decade, as the people grew more weary.

We followed the guards through the harbour, and I took advantage of the opportunity to observe my surroundings with a newfound appreciation for its magnificence. The fancier stone buildings were a pale white, having been bleached by the sun, a reflection of the baked lands they stood on. They were designed with faces that could be carved, murals of our historic battles found between open archways. Some of the older buildings were still standing on stilts, remnants of when these areas would flood. The harbour was much more developed than some villages inland, likely because of the rich trade this port once invited. I was searching for the words and the right moment to bring up the stowaway when Rimi's excited voice cut through my thoughts; she pointed to a vibrant stall along our path. We asked Nalini for permission to stop, and she granted it with a nod to the guards.

"But make it quick," she reminded us, her own attention caught by a nearby display of gold jewellery similar to what she was already wearing. We made our way over to the market stall that had piqued Rimi's curiosity, and the owner welcomed us warmly, presenting us with a beautiful yellow glass stone I would have mistaken for liquid gold had it not been so crystal clear.

"Blood of the trees, can you believe it?" he mused, twisting it so that it caught the light. Inside it, preserved in a lifelike state, was an emerald dragonfly with its wings outstretched, so real it appeared like it could have been mid-flight right there in front of us.

We both gasped in astonishment, asking him, "Where did you find this?"

He replied simply, "The Jungle."

✲✲ 18 ✲✲

As you step foot into its deep green cavernous web, the humidity engulfs you, pressing down on your throat, suffocating. The trees tower above in their shifting ascension to the skies. Their branches are so thick that they block out most of the light, leaving only a small river to illuminate the path to your deliverance. You can hear wide banana leaves being rustled in the canopy by creatures you can't see. Branches creaking and cracking under the weight of their ancestors bearing down, their judgement absolute. The steady beating of the blood in your ears. Trees seem to lean in closer to listen to your fear, feeding on it, whispering, keeping the secrets of the Jungle safe from outsiders like you. As you try to take a step, the Jungle erupts, a discordance of insects and beasts and the birds that prey on them. The ground around you trembles. Out of the corner of your eye—but past what you can see, no matter where you turn—an enormous creature thunders and breaks through the canopy. You still cannot see it. Another glimpse through the trees. Slithering towards you—

covered in spikes and scales. You still cannot see it. You know it advances.

Then you wake from the dream your teacher put in your head when you asked her what was beyond Tabashi's borders and why you weren't allowed to go there. Your best friend's hand is still in yours, and the sticky rice you stole is still stuck between your teeth.

* * *

"If I revealed all my secrets, then I'd have no shop left," the shopkeeper replied with a sly grin. We were stunned—fixed in a stare at the liquid gold pendant in his palm. "Amber" he called it.

"How much?" Rimi challenged the shopkeeper, her chin raised defiantly. The question threw me. I turned to see if she was being serious. I had spent so many days surrounded by wealth and luxury, I'd simply forgotten who I was and where I'd come from. Standing there, with the thought of being asked to produce some coins to trade with, I almost laughed. There I was, dressed in an outfit gifted by Petakai that I could never have afforded on my own, haggling over prices at a market that, on all the days leading up to these, I knew I couldn't afford to shop in. I thought of the market stall owner that I'd encountered when I first stepped foot on the docks just a few weeks ago. An entire kingdom, a proposal to a prince, and a whole encounter with a naga later—and I was still too embarrassed to produce my purse for trade. At that point, I didn't even have a purse.

"Five coins," he countered coolly.

"Five!" both of us exclaimed, unable to hold back our astonishment.

"Shi have mercy," Rimi uttered under her breath—it brought me great relief to know that five coins for a pretty stone were an inordinate amount, even for an Exorci of Tabashi.

"It's not a simple task. You wouldn't want to be stuck out there once the sun sets," he warned.

"What happens then?" I asked immediately, and Rimi squeezed my hand with fervour; the sensation felt familiar yet a world away.

Once, we would do this: dare each other to run out and touch the wide palm leaves at the Jungle's edge, just to see if we could. The great wide fronds of the place we were told we could never venture into. A game we would play before we would get told off, scolded for bringing in the dirt on our wandering feet. "Go!" we would yell together, as we raced out towards it. Our laughter ringing out across the fields. But we never quite made it. I could still hear the laughter. Reader, the memories would find me faster and more fervent now. I was back in the smells and tastes of the land where I was first cursed with them. I would always wonder if I was catching familiar voices on the wind—hearing my name, or simply going mad.

As we motioned to leave, the shopkeeper scanned our faces, and a concerning thought crossed his brow. He called out, "Wait. Don't I know you?"

I shouldn't have stopped, but my fear made me. I didn't respond. But before I could do anything else or turn to go, his hand shot out and wrapped around my wrist with a tight grip.

"I'm not from this part of town," I pleaded with panic, tugging at Rimi's robes—trying to break free from the encounter. Rimi simply shot me a look of concern. The shopkeeper didn't let go. Instead, his grip on my wrist tightened. So too the vine of guilt still wrapped around my throat. I could no longer swallow.

"You're that girl," he accused, his voice low and venomous. "That orphan girl from the school. The one that burned down."

I reached my other hand out to claw at his, trying to pry myself free from his grasp, but he called out for others to come and have a look. I could feel the water rushing in, my mind blanketed by the tides. But before the swirling storm threatened to burst open all that I had been holding in, Rimi's hand reached out to the shopkeeper's and he cried out in pain; it completely distracted me and dissipated my storm clouds, and his hand let go of my wrist. I quickly brought my hand to my chest and held onto it as if it could fall right off my body.

"Cursed Exorci!" he yelled, soothing his hands by blowing air onto them. His features furiously scrunched with bitter hatred. You could tell who Rimi was from the colour of her robes, but he must have been playing coy to get our coin. More people had gathered by then, riled and thirsty for entertainment, since true justice for their plight was too far out of reach. But just as things seemed to be spiralling out of control, Nalini appeared at Rimi's side and Alewic by mine. He placed a hand on my back, steadying me, and the guards surrounded them. I had to remind myself that they were there protecting me, that I didn't have to run. I imagined that's what it felt like to be on the side of influence—of wealth and power.

Reader, it felt dirty.

"These are guests of the royal family," Nalini said firmly. "You'll hold your tongue if you know what's good for you." I heard the gasps of spectators around us as they gathered to watch the oncoming storm, and felt the stifling compression of unwanted attention and its demand for satisfaction. Reader, I would do that man no justice to write the watered-down translations of his next words without stressing to you the importance of their true meaning. If you need a reminder, you can find one back at the beginning of the tale. There is no shame in that—I flip back the pages many times myself to look for a way back to things undiluted. I suppose it's a blessing and a curse that we can. If it is written, then the weight of it is never lost, and some things can hurt just the same—no matter how many times you read it.

"Not by blood," he hissed at us. Despite Nalini's threat. Despite the guards. I heard a murmur ripple through the marketplace, as arresting as the call of the buffalo horn. This was a phrase that I had heard many times before; it was a dangerous one. The Council considered slander treason, and treason was a crime punishable by death or exile. With a look of dismissal, Nalini led us away from the shopkeeper and back on our path towards the palace. Guards swarmed in around him. I had missed the chance to see it happen in these markets back when I first departed from them, but I could see now how the events transpired for the devout. His stone-cold gaze, what could compel someone to such fury? I looked around at the eyes that were still fixed on us and heard the judgements being shared between them. The merchant would be taken away and tried. Would anyone here stand with him? Often, charges would be dismissed when enough witnesses gathered to say that the words had never left the man's mouth. It was a game they all played—to satisfy the power and the people in equal measure. Enough entertainment to feed the greedy and enough justice to stop the hungry from rioting.

The sad thing was that it was absolutely true, what he had said. Tabashi really had no rightful ruler, and no known children born of the royal bloodline. For the king had died hundreds of years ago and the Council were ruling in his stead, refusing to relinquish the centralised control of the kingdom. Claiming that one day Anamashta will return and choose a rightful heir to the throne; that's what they taught us in all their schools: the Prophecy. But Tabashi's people had been divided since the day that we lost our great king. A fury had seeped into their hearts, hardening it with every failed crop and season without rain. It didn't matter that once the Council had done right by the people; they could never do enough good to keep up with the consequences of the Great War and its Terrible outcome.

As we walked away from the scene, I couldn't shake the vine that held my throat hostage, the lies that threatened to suffocate me before the day's end. Nor would I soon forget those eyes that burned with hate, searing his search for answers within mine. We were definitely back in Tabashi; I felt it in the dry heat of the sun and in the anger in the streets. I tried to turn to Rimi and explain what had happened, but I didn't have the words or the strength, having already spent it fighting the vine for every breath. Thankfully, she also never asked. I'd seen her turn to hide her face from me too, sitting in the shadows that lurked in her mind. I never pried either, never demanded she reveal more of herself than she was ready to. We had slowly, over the days, come to an understanding. We would offer the other the grace of time.

At the end of the harbour markets, we stopped to board a buffalo carriage that had been pulled up and was waiting for us. The carriage was adorned with elaborate regalia and flanked by a retinue of royal guards, who stood at attention with their spears at the ready.

On the other side of the road, pulling up in smoke, a similar carriage but from a decade before—one that had carried away the girl whose name I bore, a name I had promised to never forget. It stopped just ahead of us and I stopped in my tracks. Unable to keep going. Rooted to the ground as I had been then. The vision played out as vividly as the day it happened: Linh screaming as guards opened the carriage doors. The same ones that stood there now. Though, in my vision, they were made of ash. If once the guards had carried golden chains and bright human eyes, before me, they were hollow, making way for the flames. It wasn't real. It couldn't have been.

"Linh, are you alright?" I thought I heard Rimi say next to me, but her voice was a distant call. *No, she wasn't alright. She's still not alright.* Something gripped me by the shoulders and spun me. "Linh," Rimi said with force, somehow finding me in my blurred vision. The roots snapped, and I had control of my feet once more, my vision settling on the very real face in front of me. I could see the beads of sweat that had formed across her forehead.

"Yes, s-s-sorry," I stammered out and took in a laboured breath to collect myself.

"We can talk about what just happened, but let's get out of here first, okay?" she said in a voice as gentle as she could muster, but her urgency was undeniable. I looked back at the markets, at the growing crowd. Facing the carriage, the real one, built sturdier and fancier than any other, to stop myself from disappearing again, I focused on the handiwork. Intricate carvings and designs of leaves on its exterior, delicate fringes of gold hanging off the edges. On the roof was a white umbrella painted with gold embellishments and the image of Shi, providing shade from the unforgiving heat. Shi who looked at me when I was floating at the bottom of the sea.

A guard reached a hand out to me and I took it listlessly, letting my mind empty and the edges of my vision blur with it. Someone lightly guided me into my seat. My companions followed swiftly behind. I felt them sit down as it gently rocked the transport, perched on large wooden wheels, the rims visible out the windows of the carriage from inside. I had never been treated that kindly before in that kingdom and by those guards. I looked back out the other window of the carriage. I was thankful for the inordinate number of them. Despite the dreamy state I was in, I noticed the significant size of the gathering crowd. A sea of bodies growing taller the more I stared, turning into trees, a jungle canopy of their own. I tried many times to bring my mind back to the present, to the dangers that were happening around me. I thought back to what he had said, the merchant, the curse he had thrown at Rimi because of her powers. Most onlookers had faces of curiosity, but some were mixed with scorn. In a land where water was scarce and the crop catching fire meant the invaluable loss of food for a village, those who wielded the power to do so were not looked upon with mercy. I reached down to squeeze Rimi's hand but found it had been bundled into a fist. I thought about how she was treated differently in Petakai—gawked at, sure, but at least not seen as a threat.

"Why do you choose to come back here after all these years, fight in their army, if people look at you this way?" I asked, hearing great sympathy in my voice. It felt easier to come back into myself if I had someone else to worry about. I realised how much I valued our growing closeness. Not just because of how she helped me, but because of who she was, how she turned to face the world despite how it turned away from her. I wanted very much to look after whatever delicate thing we had—it was real.

"Because they need me," she replied patiently. "Their looks don't matter then."

"Plus, there's sticky rice in Tabashi," Alewic added with a brash grin. His tone was so jarring, it almost sent me back into the smoke and ash. But thankfully, instead I laughed. It was an incredible remedy. Every shadow receded, scared away by the noise. I had only the bright faces of my companions brightening my own.

"Oh! We never got some. If we pass by Kern, I can show you where to find the best of it," I replied, feeling something close to pride. It was rare that I possessed a knowledge of these lands that was familiar to me and new to others. In my new robes, in a royal carriage—with my new company. I breathed in a full breath so large it tore apart the vine. My throat was finally free.

"We're heading straight to the palace. We can't afford any detours now," Nalini warned with some regret. But she was reflecting the caution observed by the onlookers. "Curse them for putting us in this ridiculous tent. We're like sitting koi in a clear pond."

"And the herons are circling," Rimi added warily.

"Pardon me, Nalini Singh, but I don't see you walking to the palace in those shoes," Alewic teased.

I looked down at Nalini's feet. I had to cover my mouth with my hands to stop myself from laughing so unabashedly. Despite everything going on, Nalini was wearing the most exquisite—and likely expensive—pair of shoes I'd ever seen in my life. Intricately embroidered blue cloth sandals with curved wooden heels. Dainty patterns and colours that complemented her garments, completely out of place in our current circumstances. I couldn't stop the boisterous chuckle that escaped me. The sound of it filling my belly and clearing away the last of the smoke as easily as a strong breeze blowing in from the shore. The robes that had been gifted to me from Petakai were beautiful and vibrant, but they didn't fit me as well as they did my company. Under different circumstances, and if my head had been clear of memories that could unravel me, I would have found the entire experience incredible. It was nothing like my past lives in this place. Reader, it shames me to admit it, but I felt myself grow taller in those clothes, laughing under the shade of the royal umbrella, as we pulled away from the markets and out onto the open road.

✳ 19 ✳

We were making good time, rolling fields stretching out in all directions around us, crossing the golden sea. Once, centuries ago, these fields had been wetlands, flooded by the veins of a land whose waterways ran down from the fresh mountain springs to the ravenous tide at the mouth of the open sea. Then, centuries ago, these fields suffered the burning plight of a Great War, and though the fallen bodies would nourish the ground, there would be no water to wash away their sacrifice. Their angry spirits would linger. Their souls toiling here as farmers once did, waiting for the return of the rain to release them—cursing the land until they were. Those who remained would have to practise a new way to farm by digging long trenches, deep wells with irrigation channels from the trickling streams that remained, redirecting scarce water supplies to the most critically parched. The techniques were passed down, and Tabashi's people learned how to make the most out of the cracked and cursed earth they'd inherited. Each time a sewn seed miraculously made it through to the harvest, we would give thanks in the Festival of Gathering, tears watering the land as the skies once did.

We used to celebrate the coming of the wet season, with a week-long festival in honour of Shi, where citizens would throw water at each other to cleanse and cool off from the harsh slog of the dry season; it was a time when we would gather to show our gratitude and welcome a bountiful harvest. The streets would be full of lanterns and laughter, children gently pouring water into their elders' open palms out of respect, then squealing with delight as their elders then poured the water back over the children's heads to cleanse their spirits in return—and for a bit of fun. It was a time we came together, when we could be proud and we could heal. We lost so much more than just the rain when Tabashi dried up.

I had lost my mind to the rolling fields when we abruptly rolled to a stop. I looked out of the carriage window, trying to see what had caused the change of pace. Despite being in the carriage's shade, I could already feel my body responding to the heat of Tabashi's unforgiving sun. Nalini turned to our driver, her face clouded with concern.

"What's going on?" she demanded.

"It's just some fallen stacks of rice, miss," the driver replied. "We'll have it cleared in no time." She readied herself to step off the carriage.

"We have no time!" Nalini insisted and slunk back down into her seat. We were completely exposed, out there in the scorching heat, and Rimi had been right. I peeked at herons circling.

All at once, appearing like blood splattered across the golden field, I saw a group of red-dressed bandits. They were covered in crimson rags and leather armour, their faces obscured by masks. Then I remembered: the stowaway. I had been so distracted by the events in the markets and at the vision that had pulled up in smoke. I cursed myself for not remembering to warn my company about the dangers as we grasped the situation immediately; here was the Bashantu, and we were the target of an ambush. I reached for my blade, a fear gripping my hands harder than I could the hilt, but thankfully Rimi's response to the situation was faster. With lightning speed, she produced her own blade and had readied herself by the door to the carriage as a Bashantu rebel swung it open.

"She's here!" he cried out as Rimi held out her hand and set fire to his mask. He screamed and recoiled from the blaze, rushing to the ground to smother the flames. More Bashantu leapt for her from the opening created. Alewic pushed me down to the floor of the carriage and dashed to Rimi's aid by the open window beside her. From his pockets he produced a crystalline powder that he blew into the faces of the attacking Bashantu. The bandits cried out in pain, falling backwards and clawing at their faces. But then others readied themselves to lunge. A fight broke out on the side of the carriage they were on, Rimi sparring with her blade or her flames, Alewic with his powder and his fists out the window. Nalini demanded that the driver move, but she'd turned to reveal a fiendish glint in her eye—brandishing a hidden blade covered in a layer of fresh blood. The palace guard seated next to the driver had been woefully silent. Then I realised they were curled over. The driver shoved the body and it flopped to the ground—throat slit open and with a bright red fluid leaking out from the wound. Nothing could have tempered the scream that escaped my lips at the sight.

In an instant, Nalini raised her foot and slammed the heel of her exquisite blue shoe squarely into the driver's chest, sending her tumbling out and onto the other side of the road. She seized the reins as more bandits closed in, encircling our carriage. Despite the speed at which she'd readied herself to depart, we were already surrounded—the Bashantu had crept up the exposed side that I was on and I heard one climbing on the roof above us. Then I heard a pained cry from further back down the road and was almost too terrified to look. But reeling around to peer out of the back window I saw Captain Tanhchana Wardhani herself barrelling down the path towards us. As she got closer, I could see that she was astride a grey-trunked and tusked kikiriki—one of Tabashi's own—kicking its sharp talons at the bandit behind it. Reaching the carriage, she rose on her mount to confront the Bashantu that had gathered, making quick work of dispersing them.

"Thought you'd need me!" Tanh called out, as she reached up and grabbed the one on the roof, hurling them off it and tearing open a seam in the fabric in the process. The force of her fury sent the bandit rolling down the road a ways away from us, but there were still so many circling. Rimi raised her arms with a face of pained concentration and a ring of fire erupted from her outstretched hands—creating a wall between us and our attackers.

"Go! Get us out of here!" she shouted from the open doorway and gripped onto the posts beside her for balance. Nalini urged the buffalo forward with a whip of the reins and the heel of her shoe. The wagon lurched and nearly keeled over as it stumbled past the upturned bundles of dried rice stalks—now catching the flames from Rimi's summoning. The carriage creaked and swayed beneath us as we gained speed, and the fringe that had once decorated the frame and been torn off in the fight spiralling in the wind behind us and also catching alight with the growing flames of the field. We raced against their flaming claws, with Tanh riding furiously alongside the carriage on her kikiriki. Reader, I don't know if you've ever witnessed a buffalo running at full pelt, pulling a dishevelled royal carriage and flanked by a pirate atop a kikiriki, but I can assure you, we were quite the sight.

The Bashantu fell back, their clothing singed and smouldering. I had thought they would still try to advance their threat, brandishing their crude weapons and snarling, but they'd halted their assault, watching us with a cold and calculating gaze through the narrow eye-slits of their masks. The carriage driver, clothed in the uniform of Tabashi royal guards, rose from the ground aided by the Bashantu. I attempted to commit her face to memory, hoping to identify her later, but as the flames grew higher, her features faded into them. For a moment, the sight of seeing the face of a girl disappearing into the blaze was too much to bear—and I had to turn away.

We raced down the road. I was still clutching my dagger tightly where it rested in its sheath. I was desperately scanning the surrounding fields for any further threats as Alewic attempted to help me back into my seat. Glancing back, I saw towering black smoke clouds climbing with no end into a cloudless sky. An errant thought: *precious food is being lost to the fire.* I turned to Rimi in disbelief. She had helped us escape our enemy; why didn't she extinguish the blaze? Then a realisation: *she didn't know how.* It's why she never practised this magic on the ship, never created an open flame, why she always used her powders and materials. Rimi could always find the fire, but she could never put it out; it's how the world once was. The balance of an Exorci was always with an Estari—Anamashta and Moultisjka, the Great and the Terrible. I realised why Tabashi needed their Prophecy, the one who would return to fulfil it: they needed an Estari's power—Anamashta's heir—because even though there were not that many Exorci left in the kingdom, the ones we had were dangerous without an Estari to balance them, and we had been out of balance for centuries.

"Are you alright?" I heard gently beside me and turned to see Alewic's face full of sympathy. He carefully wrested my hands off the hilt of the dagger and took them trembling into his own steady palms. I hadn't realised the state that I was in. I nodded gingerly back at him, then stared out the window at the blurring fields.

"They did it on purpose," Nalini called out, quickly glancing back at us as she steered the buffalo down the path. Her once-immaculate robes billowed in the wind that raced past my face, and her perfect bun had come undone during the fight.

"What?" I asked.

"They wanted us to make a scene," Rimi said beside me. I heard the bitterness in her voice. Her face turned away in shame from the fires she couldn't contain. The fires that would eat away all that was left in the fields. It would be all the smoke the Bashantu needed to tell the people how dangerous the Exorci and the Council were, how cursed the soldiers and their agenda. I felt anger course through me and burden my heart with an unbearable weight. How could they pit the kingdom against the Exorci, especially when they had their own, on their side, protecting them? Who were the people meant to call against the creatures of the Jungle if not the Council and their army? Bashantu ruined these fields, the food for a village, all for a political statement. *Why?*

Reader, it is important to me you know that my anger was real but that it was also misplaced. I was brought up with the lessons on the Great War, the Jungle, and the Prophecy; the world was much bigger and much older than those stories. What I hadn't learnt yet was that sometimes there is a necessity for violence if the circumstances are born of it. When you finally hear someone shout, it may be after months—years—of being ignored. The Bashantu would be heard, by fire or fury; I still had so much to learn. People may have starved from the burning fields, but they were already starving. Rather than wonder how the Bashantu could commit such an atrocity, I should have been asking how the Council let a kingdom fall to such desperation.

"It's a two-day journey from the docks to the palace," Nalini called out to us from where she sat, "but we need to make it in one." She had taken the reins and would guide us for the rest of the journey. To my surprise, she was the only person familiar with the route. My gaze remained fixed out the window, feverishly surveying the rolling hills of golden stalk—eyes scanning for a sight of splattered blood.

** 20 **

The dusty rice paddies gave way to rugged terrain as we neared the border, with dense jungle foliage creeping in from the edges of the road. As we approached the trees, the air grew heavy with their humidity, and the sound of waking creatures filled our ears. There would be many dangerous roads in Tabashi that ran the length of the Jungle's border, but sometimes those were the quicker routes through the kingdom. It cost the Council too much to station guards along the path, so the only sign that you were making progress was a tall wooden post carved with inscriptions—meant to be spells—to protect the travellers. They also served as warnings of what was to come, and what to do with yourself should you hear the snapping of trees and the crunch of the undergrowth. Occasionally, when riding past, there would be a shrine. Constructed to the height of an adult with a miniature house on top of a platform, small offerings placed delicately in front of it: bowls of rice and a cup of rice wine under the smoking remnants of a burnt stick of incense. Even in scarcity, we honoured the spirits of the land with gifts, hoping they would pardon us for trespassing and waking them.

Tabashi's city and the palace within were built on the edge of the kingdom's greatest danger many centuries ago. Once a vast assembly of elegant garden homes for the nobility, the outer city had succumbed to the Jungle, and its menacing beasts, in the times of the Great War. To protect what little remained, a tall stone wall had been erected surrounding the inner city. It was now guarded by the few Exorci left in the kingdom—for the Jungle's threat never subsided. But to call the remaining city little would earn you a reputation as a pariah amongst the elite. The inner city was still a flourishing expanse of charming homes and abundant gardens, given their proximity to the damp. You would find in the walls the markets of the kingdom's most well-protected goods; they were thriving in the peace their wealth afforded. But the fact remained that what we had was only what was left. If history was to be believed, then the city of Tabashi was once an unrivalled feat of architectural excellence. The great city was a reflection of our booming trade with Petakai and the many people welcomed within its reach.

At least, that's what I had been taught. In the humble walls of a school that couldn't have been further from it all. I used to imagine being summoned to the palace one day, hailed as the chosen one. Playing games with my best friend; brandishing Anamashta's name and the status they gave her. Or else wishing I had been their missing heir all along, and one day they would come for me with their open arms to welcome me back home. Can you believe that, Reader? It took me this long to tell you because I was embarrassed to admit that I'd wanted this story since the beginning. The whims of a child abandoned from birth, dreaming that one day the world would realise they'd made a terrible mistake, that it was all just one big misunderstanding, you see? *You were loved—and wanted, always.*

But I was loved and wanted—always. I just didn't know it at the time. *"It's okay. I'll protect you,"* she would say to me—as I sang out all the air in my lungs, and leaked from my eyes and nose and mouth all the fears of being without. But she was gone, and all I had was that hole in my chest that had never stopped growing.

* * *

We'd ridden for hours, the sun beating down on us relentlessly. In the late afternoon, Nalini let us know we were approaching a good place to stop and rest, a chance for us to cool off and a chance for the animals to do the same. We all eagerly agreed, our bodies and our limbs too tired to continue, riddled with the tension that had seized us after our narrow escape. Whatever the Bashantu's intention, it had well served its purpose, and we were finally alone out there on the road. Probably for the last time in a while. Despite where we were headed, where I had always secretly wished to be invited to, my thoughts kept returning to the stowaway; I wanted to know where she was and whether she had planned that ambush. How was I to tell my companions? I was still grappling with the betrayal myself, and what if they thought worse of me because of it? What was my role in all of this? What did my powers of water mean to a kingdom starved of it?

We pulled up beside a tall signpost wrapped with a length of plaid fabric; it was a spot to rest and tie up the mounts. Someone had carved out a small area beside the road and into the trees so that we might venture into the thick to find some respite in the shade. We all eagerly dismounted from the carriage, Alewic agreeing to keep first watch.

"Linh, can you sense any water?" Rimi called out to me. I was so distracted I missed it at first. "Linh," she said again with a growing temper. My head snapped round to her attention, having never heard her temper before, and I saw her leaning against the post—looking dreadfully pale; she must have used up all of her energy starting that fire in the field. The others turned to look at me, rallying behind Rimi's suggestion. I felt eager to be useful to them, especially because I was already feeling guilty. Focusing on my breath, I shut my eyes and felt the waking night envelop me. In the brilliant blue hues of the sleeping world, I found the unmistakable trickle of water flowing downstream; it was further up the path and hidden by the trees.

"That way," I said, pointing my finger into the bush.

"Let's be quick about it," Nalini said, eying the quiet horizon. We had to tread carefully, listening out for any danger from the road or from the Jungle; we were on the border and it was a dangerous game—but there was a clearing that showed us others had tried to play too. Reader, as you can tell, despite all the warnings, our people had a tireless fascination with the Jungle, being told that we couldn't.

"You will find the traitor," Nalini said to Tanh, as she stepped down from her perch in the driver's seat. "She answers to the Council." Tanh nodded, dismounting from her own transport. She cut the ropes of the saddle and then urged the creature loose with a soft nudge. We watched as it skipped away into the trees before she flung the saddle into the undergrowth behind it. I blinked a few times to be sure of what I had just seen and thought back to the kunchuwarri being freed from the docks.

"A habit of yours?" I asked, trying to add some lightness to the situation. I was so glad to see Tanh again and so grateful for her skill in battle. There hadn't been a moment for me to thank her for how she'd helped me on my journey—but there were many times, and many thanks to be given.

"The captain has always taken the law into her own hands," Nalini said, adjusting her garments. They were still gorgeous, despite our thrilling adventures. Nalini looped her long black hair back into her signature low bun by the nape. When she'd finished, it was like they had never attacked us. How could she maintain her composure so well under such pressure?

"We were all born free under Shi's law. It was people who changed that," Tanh stated.

"It's me. I'm people," Nalini teased, as she walked past and into the cool shade. I heard Tanh hide a chuckle. I was glad they could turn to humour, even then. They must have been so used to the dangers of this life; my own had been difficult in its way for as long as I could remember, but never because of threats to it. The only battles I ever really fought were the trials of the heart and the fever of the mind. But I don't think you should compare them—our lives—to gauge who had it harder. There isn't a competition for a measure of pain; there is only a shared understanding between those burned.

"Nalini fights for freedoms too," Tanh said, after we watched Nalini disappear into the trees.

"Really?" I snapped. "Was there another meeting I missed where she didn't trade my name like stock?" The words poured out of me like water cascading off a cliff. I was helpless to stop them, despite how they left me feeling parched.

"Your name?" she challenged. "Look, it was only a matter of time before people found out about you," she said.

There was some sort of an apology in her words, despite her not owing me one at all. Biting my tongue to stop it from betraying me further, I turned back to Tanh.

"Kid, I can trust my crew because I know what motivates them," she continued. "Tabashi was always going to stake their claim on you. With Petakai's name in the mix, they'll at least have somebody else to answer to." This gave me pause. She was right, but I was still angry. Again, misplaced.

"So you're saying I should be grateful?" I said. Reader, I couldn't tell you what had come over me. We had all been through so much together, but I still had so few answers—even when the information centrally concerned me. I suppose I felt that it was time I demanded them.

"Nalini plays the long game," Tanh replied, lifting a low-hanging branch in front of the pair of us. "It's a thankless job. You just like me because I'm impatient," she finished with a wink, then stepped past me. I took in a quick breath and tamed the wave of a memory threatening to steal it. We were really doing it, heading into the Jungle. But there was no reason to worry about the dangers this time of day and on the very fringes—surely? I peered into the dark, and I hoped that they all knew what they were doing, that the signpost marking the clearing wasn't a warning erected by those who had perished trying to get rid of it.

We quickly found the stream of water, clear liquid running down the trail of fallen leaves. It was well within sight of the road and we stopped to refresh ourselves. The air was cool in the lighter part of the Jungle. We used to dare each other to run up and touch it, as if it could lash out to bite us—punishing us for trying. So many memories lingered here, and our understanding of things become very different as we get older. The stories we were taught, the warnings that came with them, somehow dim in the light of people and purposes bigger than our fears. These were just trees, and we were just travellers welcoming the shade of the canopy. But how it towered, a sleeping giant. Granting protection from the heat of the sun with an uncanny quiet. The only sounds were the ones coming from within: the water trickling downstream and the birds calling out in the distance. I let the clean air soothe my worries and shut my eyes to feel it completely. The humidity was a welcome respite for the lungs that had been breathing in the dry burn of the parched lands we'd ridden across. Gathering around the stream, I noticed Rimi wringing out a cloth stained like the ones worn by the Bashantu. She was cleaning her blade.

"When did you learn to fight with that?" I asked, garnering some attention from the group.

"When I became an Exorci—in the palace," she answered evenly.

"The one we head to now," Nalini shot back at me with significant force. "For someone from these parts, you sure ask a lot of questions about them." I steeled myself against her inquisition. Nalini hadn't mentioned the commotion at the marketplace. I had no way of knowing what she'd overheard, but she would need me to be on my best behaviour if she was to sell me to the kingdom with relative success. I felt a familiar storm brewing, surrounded by all the water I'd need to let it pour.

"It's been a long day. Let's not tire ourselves out before the actual fight," Tanh ordered with her captain's voice, as she finished cleaning her own blade. But I was gripping the small one at my side, my gift from Rimi, one that I still hadn't used. Admittedly, because I didn't know how. I had survived for so long by not asking too many questions and not starting any fights. Staying out of everyone's way. Disappearing when I felt myself recognising too many faces. Those who noticed how little I came with and how little I knew. But there I was, on the other side of my best efforts to vanish, my desire for anonymity unable to render me into non-existence. I could feel myself changing. Slowly, over those days, but it had added up. Maybe I too was becoming impatient.

Nalini quickly stood and made her way back to the carriage. Rimi sent a sympathetic smile my way and followed purposefully behind her. Her strength returned. I went to help myself up from the ground when Tanh reached her hand out to me instead. I took it, grateful.

"Captain," I started, as she easily hoisted me onto my feet. "Tanh, you have a good heart. I know you do."

"But?" she returned without missing a beat. I figured it was too late to hold back the question that had been burning in my mind since our encounter with the naga.

"You were so willing to sacrifice Rimi on the ship that night," I mumbled, "forgive me, but . . . I don't know how to trust you."

"Nalini knows the sacrifices she made to get to her position. She doesn't know the ones I make to keep her there. If I lose the ship, I lose her," she said to me without hesitation. I thought I was ready for anything—for her to reach out and plunge her machete right into my chest, yell at me, break her fist across my face. But I wasn't ready for the wholehearted truth, for her to be so forthright with it.

"You want trust?" she added assuredly, after I met her with my stunned silence. "Learn people's weaknesses. It's more useful."

"Nalini?" I pressed for confirmation, feeling very brazen. Tanh matched my cheeky expression.

"Stay on her good side—you won't see my bad one."

"I can't say I'm surprised. I see how you two look at each other," I said.

"Look, kid, I'd wager they all know. But I'd cut their throats if they asked," she smirked, and a nervous giggle fell out of me in response. Perhaps out of fear—but definitely out of respect.

"How is it enough for you? This double life?" I added quickly, before we got back to the others. Before it all changed. I realised this was possibly my last chance to really get to know Tanh, before she was Captain Tanhchana Wardhani of the *Bayanihan*—again.

"A double life? You're speaking to a pirate," she said with a bold grin. "A secret affair with a powerful and beautiful woman—and the biggest ship I've ever seen at my command? I'd say I'm spoiled rotten."

* * *

We let Alewic have some time to himself in the shade of the trees before we all climbed back into the carriage. We couldn't afford to let our guard down again. Peering at the others' serious faces, I readied myself for the rest of the journey. We were on the last stretch towards the palace, closer to the centre of power and the heart of the struggle for control in these devastated lands. I had to be ready for whatever lay ahead, for whatever they would ask of me. The wheels of the carriage turned, and I lost track of time. My mind found comfort in the straw-covered hills with the lives I used to live between them.

I saw them of course, running through the fields: the two girls who would never let me forget. Their laughter, music on the wind, their voices brought to me by the breeze. Reader, despite how long it is taking me to tell this entire tale, I could never take long enough. It always felt too much to handle, but I will also never stop wishing for more moments. To be there again, to linger with the people that I would miss the most, the ones I needed the most. A part of me writes this tale for myself, to turn back the pages, because I need to know that it was all worth it. That all the days that passed and the hurt that remained, that it was all headed towards something. Otherwise, why? Why did it have to hurt so much? Flipping them over, again and again, trying to pour meaning into the words, to where it all makes sense, to where I can say, *yes, this is why*. It had to happen that way, why I had to feel so lonely, and for so long. It was just lonely, never alone.

* * *

As we approached the walls of the palace, its towering presence striking a chord of warning against any encroaching creature, I gazed out of the eyes of a poor village girl who had always dreamed of becoming a princess. The skies darkened to a coal-fire black as we fell into the night, riding well past what was reasonable for a carriage bound for the palace. The darkness made the walls appear taller than they ever could have in the day. Shadows cast from the flames licked the base of the columns, creeping up and over them and beyond what we could see. Racing through the city's entrance, I saw a collection of makeshift huts and marketplaces closed up for the night. But some villagers were still awake, waving back at us with ecstatic glee, their faces filled with awe at the sight of our carriage; it was a marked difference to the faces we had passed at the harbour. I guessed the kingdom felt different this close to the inner city, its concentration of wealth; who would dare speak up against the Council here?

Two giant sculptures of dual-trunked elephants fast approached us, standing on either side of the grand entrance to the palace grounds. Buildings layered with intricacies, bannered by colourful flags that fluttered in the evening breeze. Guards lined the perimeter and stood at attention, their spears at the ready as we approached the open archways and then passed swiftly through them. The few decorations left on our carriage permitting our passage.

We entered a grand courtyard. The lingering sounds of the city at night were muffled by a second ring of high walls, creating an eerie silence that blanketed us like a low-hanging cloud. The clacking hooves of our carriage's ox and the wheels on the cobblestone were the only noises to cut through the numbing silence. The palace was more impressive up close, a sprawling complex of buildings and gardens littered with fountains carved with the image of the naga. Feeling my breath coming in short bursts, I willed time to stop, wanting to take in every detail of the moment. There had been a time when I had thought of only this, but now it was all coming at me with too much speed. In front of the heavy double doors leading into the palace were twin sculptures of fierce and wide-faced tigers, their marble eyes reflecting a circle of light that moved to follow you wherever you looked. With the torches that flickered, I could have sworn I saw them blinking.

Guards met us where we'd stopped at the entrance, and they helped us off the carriage. Having been riding for so long, I found myself unsteady on my feet and was grateful for the support, though no one who helped us returned my smiles of gratitude. Supposing I would have to get used to the courtesy of others as my status changed, I felt in my throat a stone I hadn't meant to leave there—swallowing to force it down. Nalini moved forward with silent grace and we all trailed in line behind her, guards flanking. They led us through the doors. I saw stone walls speckled with gold leaf, the ceilings high and ornate with vivid scenes from the ancient Great and Terrible battles. The air was thick with incense and jasmine, heavy with echoes in the chamber. The steady clack of Nalini's heels on the wooden floors. Lush garden ponds out of the open corridors with decorated archways pointing down like teeth. The mouth of the naga and a sky full of stars. Trickling in the fountains. Pond creatures buzzing. Grotesque displays of water in a land so parched. What Petakai had boasted with marble, Tabashi did with the only resource we couldn't live without. Columns hurtling past us. I tried counting them but quickly lost my rhythm. Peeking through the gaps, bright pink lotus flowers at the edge of my vision.

Illuminated by candlelight. Their scent rushing in to meet us. The colours streaking across my vision—like a wet painting turned over too soon. We were walking so fast. Why were we walking so fast? I turned to Rimi, seeing as we would not get another moment alone.

"Rimi," I said as quickly and as quietly as I could—cursing myself for my ill timing.

"Yes?" she whispered back to me with the same fervour, thinking it very fun—clearly.

"You haven't asked me about what happened at the markets," I said, almost like a demand.

"Yes," she replied steadily—warily.

"Well, I'm sure you have questions," I stated with more force, surprising myself. Maybe I wanted her to know. Maybe I needed someone else to.

"Now?" she countered, almost laughing.

"If not now, then when?" I cried, breaking. I had to stop myself from collapsing. It was all happening too quickly, all that change. Once we passed through another set of doors and another, who knew who else I would become? What other names would they call me? I had been running so far and for so long that when I finally stopped to turn around, I couldn't see anything behind me. I realised how alone I was in it all. If you leave everything behind, then you'll eventually find yourself with nothing to hold. I left my body there with Rimi as my mind dove into the ponds we'd rushed past, trying to escape the fire that blazed. Everyone had stopped walking, but I barely noticed. My chest was forgetting to breathe. Nalini, Alewic, and Tanh had stopped a few paces ahead, but they let us keep our distance. I noticed the guards did not gesture to usher us onwards—a small kindness. But they did not break their stare; they fixed their focus on us, on me. Rimi took her time replying, resting a steadying hand on my shoulder.

"Linh," she began carefully, trying to find me back in my body. I almost choked at the mere mention of that name; it pushed me further out into the blue. Rimi continued, "In all the days you've known about my mother, you've never once asked me to explain it." I wasn't sure what she meant. My vision blurred. She squeezed my shoulder hard. I realised she was pushing air into my sails, trying to help me lift them. "When I'm around you, I don't have to fight for my truth," she said. "You don't make me explain. I just feel believed," she finished. Finally able to catch my breath, thanks to her efforts, I breathed it in fully and let the sensations pull me back in.

"Me too," I mumbled shakily. "It's nice to have a friend who understands magic."

"It's nice to have a *friend*," she countered—and so I understood. A friend. What it meant to have her there; why the hole had never closed. I had let go of my legs all those years ago when I had lost the only thing that was helping me to hold them, and I hadn't let anyone else pull me back together again. I thought maybe it meant I would betray her, letting someone else try—but I finally realised that I was only hurting myself. Even she wouldn't have wanted that. I owed it to her—at least. But really, I owed it to myself.

"Lahela," I breathed.

"What?" Rimi asked.

"My name. That's my name," I stammered through a cracking voice. "Lahela. Lahela Tabashi. I just needed you to know it. I need someone to remember."

"Lahela," she repeated it back to me. No hint of betrayal, no fear of the truth. To have it held with such regard—I almost cried.

"Ready?" I heard from Nalini ahead. I looked up to lock eyes with her piercing gaze full of genuine sympathy, a feeling they all shared. Alewic, Tanh, Rimi—we had all come here together. I straightened up and nodded with all the bravery that I could muster, that they had shown me, and we continued down the hall. More candles started catching fire. I turned to Rimi and saw her face tense up. I finally remembered that there would be other Exorci there in the palace. Flames successively appeared down the corridor. My vision blurred as we walked. Then, finally, we arrived at our destination—another council room, but in a different kingdom and with more distrustful looks directed at me. They had padded the hard wooden floors with textiles and cushions, and silks lined the walls and ceiling. There they were, seated cross-legged on a large embellished wooden platform at the end of the room: the Council. I took a deep breath, trying to calm my nerves. I hadn't realised they would be awake and ready to meet us.

"Welcome," a woman said, gesturing for us to approach. We showed courtesy by following Nalini's cues, bowing our heads, then bringing ourselves to the floor. I looked up at the woman who had welcomed us in. She was seated at the centre of the platform on her own decorated bench, raised higher than the other members—the head of the Council. Her eyes were like the night sky; her hair was like the clouds that filled it.

✲✲ 21 ✲✲

I won't try to figure out what was real and therefore worth explaining. I think it was all real—especially what I can't explain—so instead I will just tell you what I saw: twin moons sinking beneath the tide; the eyes of the naga and a mouth full of stars becoming a face, becoming a sun; over a field with two girls running to reach each other before the Jungle reached them first, and before the fire engulfed them; like twin suns in the midst of the inferno. The oxen, bellowing and racing across the field towards them, ready to lunge, a thousand of them in suits of armour reaching, and she stands before them, arms raised. She is on fire, and her eyes are a storm, and she is the dark clouds and I am the rain, and she is falling into the stars and I am caught in the swell, pulled into the ocean, and I can't see her through the currents as they envelop the sun. The last thing I hear in the deafening sea is her laughter, buffering me like the waves. I gasped, air filled my lungs, and I awoke. The dawn broke against my body—shivering—as I lay in my bed, wet from my panic. My hands were as clammy as the rest of my skin as I wrapped them around my chest—as if my arms were the only things that could keep me from collapsing—and I reminded myself, *Lahela. Lahela Tabashi. I am real—and I am here.*

Reader, when you are born into a soft world, on a soft bed, with soft hands to wipe your face should you find them dampened, then time and memory will flow smoothly like the river on its course from the sky to the sea. Well, this was my river, and my riverbed—shaped by drought and storm; it was why I had tried to flee Tabashi to start anew and why, after entering the palace and meeting the Council, I simply sank beneath the water, tired from fighting the rapids. All light and sound was dampened, and my body was one with the waves. I only surfaced days later, sitting up in that expensive bed, wading through my own fears and trying to regain myself—the most present I had been in almost a week. Caught up, I could hear children laughing outside my bedroom. I reached for that sound—something real—and upon realising that, my breathing finally settled back into a rhythm that let me rise. *Lahela Tabashi. I am Lahela Tabashi. I am back in the dry lands—awake, in my room in the palace, ready for the dawn of a new day.*

If I looked out of the window, its carved wooden frame like vines climbing up the trunk of a tree, I could see the Jungle far off into the distance and beyond the thick stone walls that guarded the city. The wind swirled through the leaves to create a churning sea of deep green. From that distance it looked so peaceful, its canopy appearing so soft you could lie across it—it was also still waking—so different in the dawn's light that my fears about it seemed childish and a whirlpool away.

Across the morning mist were the barren fields and the houses that sat on stilts amongst them. Bamboo and rattan and straw as far as the eye could see. Gingham garments were draped across branches and hung out to dry amidst baskets of fish and fruit. Oxen woke up to the call of their farmers ready to plough the fields with them. I had missed these lands without realising it, a stark contrast to the ones in Petakai. From the ocean to the sea of rice to the Jungle—it's amazing the view that a new perspective can give you.

The walls of my bedroom were covered in murals of the Great and Terrible battles: famed serpents and oxen chasing Anamashta into the Jungle; a giant black monkey wrestling with a serpent between its teeth; two golden kikirikis flying off with one in its talons, then throwing it into the mouth of the naga rising from the sea; soldiers gathered by the thousands.

Shaking off the last of the mist collecting behind my eyes, I strayed from the walls that had found their way into my dreams last night—likely because I was spending too much time in that room staring at them. Large windows framed with sheer curtains fluttered in the gentle breeze wafting in from outside, carrying with it the sweet scent of blooming lotus flowers, mixing with the smells from the vases of fresh ones already in my room. Delicate porcelain cups and saucers sat on a small table by the window. I'd never held porcelain before, *I, Lahela Tabashi*. Finally able to hear the sounds of a trickling fountain outside.

As if on cue, I heard a gentle knock on the door. I shakily climbed off the bed. My feet sank into the soft textile rug covering the wooden floors of the bedroom. To explain wealth, I'd describe it as justifying hours of delicate handiwork for something to be trampled on by feet, the lowest and dirtiest parts of our bodies. I remembered a time when shoes were my greatest luxury. They were still so uncommon in most parts of Tabashi, even for the nobility. Brought over on the ships from Petakai. Part of me would always still love the sensation of my bare feet against the dirt. I'd seek it out when my mind was wandering down an errant stream and I needed it caught. Perhaps today I could find time to visit the garden, sinking into the soft grass and seeing if I could feel Shi through it.

I quickly made my way over to an ornate dresser in the room to throw on something that wasn't damp from my fears. I replaced my bed sarong with a plain cotton one that I wrapped around my chest, using another length of fabric to wrap around my waist and tuck into my waistband. When I was decent, I called for the maiden to enter. She came in dressed in simple cotton wrappings the colour of the earth and kept her head low, making her way over to the wardrobe and retrieving my garment for the day's proceedings. She silently brought the royal gown to me and I lifted my arms so that she could wrap it around my body. I watched the image of Shi, and the energy that flowed from her into the water, as it curled around my collarbone. Reader, I've realised I never explained: Shi is the original source of power in Isira, the first woman. Her body is the land that we live on and her magic is creation—it exists in all things and becomes our present to cherish. We must tend to her as the crew to the penjajap, as soldiers to their machetes. On the carefully embroidered silk, her head hung close to my heart, with her trailing magic pleated and draped over my shoulder.

When the maiden had finished, she ushered me over to a bronze mirror leaning against a corner of the room to have a proper look. I saw the quaint figure of a timid girl: tanned skin, a fragile frame, long black hair dripping like ink down a page. She had the solemn demeanour of a nervously quiet village cat, having witnessed their kind being chased out with a straw broom one too many times; all they wanted was some fish from the rivers that we had emptied. I felt much closer to the girl who had dressed me, her head hung low as she stood back, than the richly outfitted one staring back from the mirror. I often avoided them, and the thoughts they inspired, worried that if I looked too long and too close the image might vanish into smoke. Shaking off a feeling I couldn't name, I tried my best to make the image look taller, rolling the shoulders and lifting the chin, the weight of the garment becoming very apparent. *I am Lahela of Tabashi.*

That name had disappeared with the records of a school that burned down. Introducing myself to the Council had stirred no interest above what we'd already presented: my Estari magic and the chance at fulfilling the Prophecy. There were other ways to explain my lack of a title, and the Council weren't interested in hearing them, whatever the case, so used to changing girls' names as it suited them. But I was *of* Tabashi because someone had given me to its care. It wasn't easy, Reader, to hold that title; but if nothing else, I could at least own my suffering. Lahela Tabashi it was, and—it seemed—Estari too.

The ringing of a gong pulled me from my thoughts. The children that I'd heard laughing earlier stopped their fun to search for the source of the noise. I followed their flight to the citizens and villagers who were gathering in the thousands out the front of the palace. They had all arrived in their finest, dressed in sompot and sarongs using the fabric I had seen hanging out on the branches that same morning. They were there for the Festival of Gathering, a time when all the different people of our kingdom would come together to share and celebrate their different cultures, presenting their hard-earned harvest with songs from their land and food prepared with their family's secret recipes. Music filled the streets: bamboo flutes and gamelan percussion, rallied by the excited claps and cheers from the crowd. This harvest season, we had more reason to rejoice; the timing couldn't have been more fortuitous. Today we would celebrate the second coming of Anamashta the Great, her prophesied successor—by order of the Council, on behalf of the King.

For all you know, this is Anamashta's heir, sang out a voice in my mind. It was coming from the Council. The memory found me like a flood. Even awake, I would have no choice in being pulled back into that room. Such is the nature of the river, Reader, and you will have to bear with me on its course. I was introduced to all the members of the inner circle of leadership in Tabashi that evening, their names washing over me like the ones that had circled around Petakai. I almost thought that I'd never left, that I was still trapped under the sea and in a room of my worst nightmares, caught in the swell where people spoke about—but never to—me.

"Impossible," replied Seriatha Navindi, the woman who led the Council to rule over Tabashi. The sight of her dark clouds still pierced mine from when she had first welcomed us into the fire-lit halls. She wore a rich purple wrap embroidered with silver thread, and a pleated black silk sash was thrown over her shoulder. Her outfit had a similar extravagance to the other council members, but nobody else wore Seriatha's colours—save for Rimi's black robes—and Seriatha's jewellery was much, much finer.

"It's true," the captain confirmed. "I saw her powers with my own eyes."

"Anamashta's bloodline ended with her hundreds of years ago," Seriatha collected, her tone impassive. She would not betray her thoughts, nor would anyone else on the Council. I thought they might have been more relieved that I was an answer to their prayers, the deliverer of the Prophecy. This was their promise: that they would play warden to the seat of the throne, holding the uncontested power of royal lineage until a rightful heir should arise to claim the title. Their vision of a Great Tabashi—the return of the rain—was taught in all the schools that the Council had built to educate us on it. Anamashta's power would come back to these lands, and the greatest way to show our gratitude was to patiently wait for it, through fire and drought. A hundred years had passed without a cloud in the sky, another hundred without rain; the rivers dried up, the stocks ran low, and farm animals withered like the people who cared for them. In another hundred we would forget the names of the people who fought in the Great War, forget the reasons that had kept us placid through all those seasons without change; it's amazing how hunger gets passed down through the generations. Hope eventually turned to despair, and despair to rage.

When the Eyrell burned down, I ran—without memory, and without a friend. Another fire and another field gone, the debts of our lands—long overdue—could no longer be tempered with the promises of a bygone era. The people who had made them were already gone, having passed into the loving embrace of Shi; they would never go thirsty again. For those who remained, there would be payment—with grain or with blood. So I ran, not knowing who chased me, but afraid that they might find me and take what was due.

"Will that be all?" the maiden said to me, her voice barely above a whisper as I fell out of the river and back into my body in the room. *I am Lahela Tabashi. I am real, and I am here.*

Reader, I would be in two places that day. In the present, waiting for the evening's festivities, and in the past with the Council, a few days before they had announced them. Though I could just tell you these things in sequence, as they happened, that would do no justice to how they made sense. In trying to recount my story, I pick up a glass jar and pour the entirety into my open mouth; if I go too fast, the water rushes, splashing out and away and escaping my thirst for knowing it. To put it simply, being in that room with the Council was too much, and I could only muster the strength to do so in the days following. To be moulded and made, and made again, by others' hands—sometimes you just have to sink beneath the tide until the storm passes. It's why I tell it to you like this, in fragments. This is how it had to happen for me too, how I weathered the storm and their hands, how I survived drinking from the jar once I realised the water was poisoned.

"Yes, thank you," I replied to the maiden, offering as much warmth as I could. She bowed her head and left the room. But as she lifted her face to close the door, a flash of recognition crossed mine; the sediments often pooled at the base of my thoughts were already disturbed, floating about and ready to be caught with the current. A memory surfaced—of the Eyrell, and the girl being pulled into a carriage screaming.

"Wait!" I called out too late; she'd shut the door. I ran over and threw it open, revealing only Rimi; she was standing alone in the hall. Her face lit up.

"Good morning, Lahela!" she exclaimed with such jarring force that it sent a wave onto the sediment to clear it. I hadn't heard that name for so long, I couldn't help the smile that came to the call. I looked around one last time for the maiden, but had to resign myself to the river's new course. Rimi needed no more reasons for concern, and I could always find smoother currents guided by her hand. We all had expectations on us that day, the pressures of a kingdom that had waited centuries for some good news.

It would be breakfast soon, and nothing comforted my mind like a full belly—the things about us that never change. There was always plenty of food in the city; it was something else that I would never get used to—though a part of me wanted to. Each morning, Rimi had met me at my chambers; so, without waiting for a response, she set off across the lush but well-manicured grounds. I followed close behind—a village girl wandering around the palace in the costume of a princess.

"What was it like then, growing up here?" Rimi asked openly; she must have been continuing a conversation we'd had in the days prior.

"I try not to think about it," I replied, a half-truth; the memories always came against my will. The only way I'd found to have a choice in the matter was to never mention, or even think about, their names. Linh's was the only truth I allowed myself to hold, because I'd promised to. I try to leave everything else undisturbed, lest the skies should open up for the rains to pour. The girl whose name had the power to hurt the most I guarded as if my life depended on it. Her face, and her eyes, would torture me enough. If Linh and the Eyrell could bring on a downpour, I imagined my best friend's name could bring about a flood that would cover all the lands in Isira.

"I'm sorry. It can't have been easy," Rimi said carefully. It made sense that when I finally told her my real name she wanted to know more about where it had come from. How could I tell her my name was all I could give her? Despite everything we had been through together, I could not quickly overwrite the hurt of the past with kindness. I simply continued on my course, the river joined by a newfound stream—warmer water mixing with the cold.

"You find your fun when you're a kid. We always tried to."

"You and—?"

"Friends," I said quickly, "at school." But I never named the school. "We would go around stealing sticky rice until we got caught."

"And what would happen then?" she asked.

"Oh the usual, a quick beating with a straw broom and we'd be on our way—up to cause more trouble."

"Shi have mercy."

"What? What did I say?"

"Beating?"

"Oh, not like that," I shot back, but I'd stopped walking. "All the teachers did, didn't they?"

"No, Lahela, they didn't. They shouldn't," she said urgently.

"Not even your parents?" I asked, trailing off.

"Lahela?" Rimi asked softly. "We can change the subject."

But I was already off again, running through the fields of drying rice, the tide washing over the sun.

✳ ✳ 22 ✳ ✳

Drums from the streets of the city reached us through the ground, like a heartbeat of the land. It was like it was Shi herself who brought me back into my body that time. The citizens of Tabashi were singing their proud anthems and the air that wafted in from the balconies carried their charge; you can't deny the energy of hope. It had been so long since we had truly come together, united, to celebrate the times. If only the entire kingdom could have bathed in the riches offered by the palace gardens, then maybe we could have come together much sooner. How simple it must have been for the Council, ensconced in luxury's embrace, to linger here, proclaiming salvation while they themselves had already crossed the threshold. I considered the part that I must play in the stories the Council would weave: the tale where Anamashta's heir opens up the sky and centuries of rain pour down to quench the thirst. I looked down at my hands, seemingly too small for the monumental task that lay ahead, and shifted uncomfortably in my fine silk garments, feeling as though I had yet to truly earn the luxury they afforded.

The wooden doors of the palace sighed open as royal guards marched out in practised harmony, their footsteps like the city's drums through the hallowed halls of the palace. They were followed by the decorated palace procession. Banners hung between the archways that encircled the buildings, the bright hues mirrored in the Council's garments. They all felt as much a part of this place as its foundations. When you've only heard about them, the people in charge, it's easy to muster contempt—a bitter anger for the wealth they hoarded in a kingdom so desperate, and so deserving of more. But being there, Reader, with the promise to one day be part of it all—I would be lying if I said I hadn't yearned for it too sometimes, with all the ache of a child who dreamt of greatness in excess—of safety offered unconditionally. I did not know how wrong I could be.

Wardhani? That's a good title. Your ancestors fought in the war. Is that how you became our penjajap's captain? Seriatha asked, her voice crashing into my mind. She had many questions about our company that night: who was on the *Bayanihan*, who sat on the council at Petakai, and which of the Tamaravati royals sat in the audience chamber.

"Amongst other reasons," Tanh replied collectedly, another hand gesture to Nalini. "Wardhani" was the title of a war hero, the first woman to fight, and die, protecting our king, back before they allowed women to fight, before they realised we had been fighting anyway, with bandages and sewing needles. Tanh's title belonged to a legacy that may not have been part of the aristocracy but offered an inheritance of respect. That one noble act of Wardhani's defiance earned her family's title a place in history.

"You honour us, Captain," called out a member of the Council from behind a golden mask with the face of a monkey curled into a smile. It was unnerving.

"Azmi," Seriatha continued her study of us, "your family's legacy precedes you. How is the university?"

"Excellent, and in the capable hands of my nephew in my absence, Navindi," Alewic answered with a steady tone, revealing nothing. He addressed her by her title, as did all the members of the Council. I wondered if that's what titles afforded you: a casual comfort amongst the elite when your titles date back to the times of the Great War. I could have argued that Tabashi was the oldest title in the room, but I didn't think I'd find any allies with that claim.

Since I was already watching Nalini for the secret conversation she was having with the captain, I saw her response to Alewic's remark; it had caused a twitch in the vein in her neck where she must carry the stress of protecting him from their kingdom. Almost as if she knew, Seriatha turned to Nalini.

"And what of this—"Singh"? I don't recognise it. How did you come to be in this position?"

"I'm the first in my family to graduate," Nalini replied.

"So they let anyone lead now?" Seriatha said darkly.

"With respect, Seriatha, I earned my rank," Nalini said too quickly and with too much sharpness in her tone. Nalini's use of Seriatha's name—and not her title—would not go unnoticed.

"Singh outperformed her peers by a landslide. She was a clear first choice, Navindi," Alewic hurled back, but it was too late to temper the curse.

"But she wasn't chosen, was she? Petakai's laws prevent it," Seriatha declared.

"No, I wasn't," Nalini fought back. "The position was a gift in recognition of my dedication to—"

"Then why has it taken your family so long to claim a seat at the table? If they're as capable as you say?"

"Well, your closed doors don't make it easy."

"Ah, there it is—the etiquette of a girl with no title." And there it was, the pretence of those who bear them. I hadn't known that Nalini's family wasn't from nobility, but from that moment on, everything about her became clear. *Nalini fights for freedoms too,* the captain had said. I felt in my heart the greatest of sympathies for the trials she had to have endured, and that she continues to endure, to make up for being born too clever in a world that chooses institution over excellence. How was it that Wardhani's actions endowed her descendants with reverence, yet Sing's was met with contempt? I suppose that only time could tell if any of us would become a Great, or a Terrible.

TAPESTRIES OF A KINGDOM

* * *

Rimi and I stepped onto the balcony of the palace's central courtyard, decorated galleries and mezzanines that overlooked the garden, but our attention was caught by a full-grown mother elephant, beside her wrinkly grey baby, dressed in gleaming gold jewellery and vibrant flowing drapes. We watched in awe as she playfully offered warm sticky rice on banana leaves to the giggling company seated and waiting at the edge of the gallery, the elephant's trunk outstretched with familiar grace. They must have trained it for this exact purpose: to serve food for the Council's retinue, adding unnecessary extravagance to the simple act of eating breakfast. It all felt so unbelievable, and was probably why I so easily drifted in and out of a dream-like state. Here they had enough food for themselves, and in so much excess as to justify entertainment with it. How was this the same kingdom that I'd grown up stealing sticky rice in? Rimi and I exchanged wary glances as we drifted towards the others, joining them on plush floor cushions.

Laughter and conversation swirled around us as we savoured the food. Served mostly by human hands—but now and then by a dexterous grey trunk. I was lulled by the smoky allure of the meal: grilled pork skewered on bamboo, warm ginger-infused rice congee, and fresh garden-picked fruits of rambutan, mangosteen, and jackfruit.

Around us were handmaidens and royal companions arrayed in opulent and embroidered garments that left their midriffs bare. Guards stood nearby, their presence a subtle reminder of the world beyond this moment of enchantment—of policy and of wars.

"How was it studying at your father's university?" I asked Rimi.

"Vatthana's?" she corrected me. "I didn't mind it. I could have continued, until . . ." she drifted off solemnly. Our company was distracted by their own conversation, but I still regretted stumbling into this one for Rimi; maybe we were both still not ready to give more than our names, but there was friendship to be found in patience. Reader, for the things that matter, wait; it is always worth it.

"I joined the Council's army as soon as I was old enough, much to my father's dismay," Rimi said.

"Old enough? But then . . . you must have still been a child when you started at the university," I gasped.

"I was their best student, well, second, of course, to Nalini. But she'd had a head start," Rimi added playfully.

"But with your family's title, surely you could have ended up with a seat on the high council?" I asked.

"Perhaps," she said with such finality that I felt it rude to pry. Considering names and their adjacent titles, my mind wandered down a bubbling stream.

TAPESTRIES OF A KINGDOM

* * *

"It's our records, Navindi, our word. All they would need is her title." Flames flickered in the low-lit halls as the Council pressed their charge. Despite how they reminded me of Petakai, those Tabashi halls were darker, the ceiling seemed closer, and their voices were harsher. Their faces, ones that weren't behind masks, were as cold and unmoving as the dark wood that surrounded us. Rimi had tried to speak up, to come to my defence, but they shut her down faster than the child who runs home for fear of the dreadful night. I thought I had been powerless before; I would be wrong many times before the night was over.

"Anamashta's heir is the closest thing we've come to a royal bloodline in centuries," they said.

"We will not sully Anamashta's name with a commoner," Seriatha replied in a measured tone. There were many talks, and many more arguments—parries of names and who to blame for the victimless crimes I had committed by stepping into my power, raised voices and orders for what price to put on actions taken without their consent. Nalini had presented Petakai's offer: that Prince Tamaravati, of the royal Tamaravati bloodline, would take the Estari's hand in marriage—my hand—if they could prove my powers and authenticate a claim to Tabashi's throne. I recalled the sterile conditions in which I had met the prince, the loveless affair. If the Council could prove that I was worthy of the title, make the passage across the sea safely, and bring back the rain, they could consider their debts paid. A gift of matrimony from Petakai and the kingdoms would forge an enduring alliance once again.

The offer caused an outcry; it was an attack on the Council's pride. Fury found me easily then; they were arguing because of vanity. It was laughable, but their decisions would damn the real lives of the people, those who depended on the Council to not equate egotism with principles. With no way to spend my rage, I drifted out of that room and into any current that would take me. That night I found the flicker of a lit torch in the corner and I disappeared into it like the smoke that curled, its flames dancing their way into my dreams—dancing its way into the sun.

23

Blazing down overhead as we ate and drank, marking the approach of noon. Farmers had finished their work for the morning and returned their oxen to graze. Views of their bony spines against a pale expansive backdrop left me feeling guilty for the food I'd indulged in all morning. Sun-scorched straw reeds swayed listlessly in the breeze as dogs wandered in search of food between the villagers—who chased them out. In our kingdom, we were meant to live in close harmony with all creatures, revering them as creations of Shi with souls just like our own, crafted with the same loving touch. But as the soil dried up, so did the good temperament of tenderness; this was no longer a world for soft things and their soft beings. This was the world that I had grown up in, the world that the Council decided for, despite how little their decisions affected them—here up high. But I too was no longer down there amongst the people; I was in the palace, lounging on cushions and enjoying light refreshments of sweet coconut water and delectable sweets—served on the trunk of an elephant. If I had been any more than the person I was, perhaps I could have done something; but things were already being done, by people I admired who were much greater than me. I hoped to join them one day, Reader; I just didn't yet know how.

We had been there all morning, playing games across the table by counting small wooden balls rolled across it. Sometimes it led to playful disagreements, so I preferred to watch, too slow to pick up the rules, to be fast enough to counter. I had to remind myself that my company and I had learnt to count for very different reasons: rationing water to last without the promise of rain.

". . . and this morning, while I was fetching the bananas, a bright orange arm swung at me!" I heard beside me, pulling me from the sea.

"An orangutan?" someone else asked.

"Just so! Apparently, I was the one who was where I shouldn't be," they said, finishing their tale with the tilt of their head to cue polite laughter; it was a sound I'd perfected over the many similar meals I was expected to attend. *It's a fair trade*, I thought, washing down my lies with the coconut water and bringing another pork skewer to my lips; but I could not wash down the shame of my indulgence. I doubted I would ever get used to the feeling. *Lahela Tabashi—that's who I am. A village girl with no title.*

Just then, two vibrantly coloured birds with lengthy tail feathers swooped down and nearly pilfered our meal, plunging our company into a whirlwind of genuine squeals and laughter. Even the palace guards struggled to conceal their amusement as their expressions softened at the edges. There was nothing more joyous than unbridled freedom, and even here in the palace there was fun to be found in their blatant disregard of formalities; the residents' would not have such freedoms. As the staff busied themselves with preparing the lunch area, I felt eager to stretch my legs and get away from the conversations and games that I struggled to partake in. I was painfully full from the morning's privileges; I had eaten many times the amount of the others, forgetting that I could stop because there would always be more. Rising delicately and turning to Rimi's inquisitive glance, I went to ask her if she would join me on the balcony when a palace guard interrupted me.

"Rimisin Azmi," the guard beckoned, thoughtfully placing his request in the lull that had settled. Fortune permitted at least one of us to take part in the secret meetings, and I swallowed the frustration of being left with the others. This wasn't a pleasant experience for either of us. Rimi politely took her leave.

"Let me know how it goes," I called ineffectively behind her, then willed myself to make the most of my time with her gone—somehow.

The palace corridors stretched out into the abundant gardens. I drifted past the palace staff, their heads dipping gracefully in deference, and I returned the gesture timidly—still unfamiliar with the dance of courtly etiquette. Peering across the kingdom from the balconies, devouring the sights as ravenously as my belly had been for breakfast, I'll admit, I felt small, and terribly frightened. The city roared with festive charm in celebration of the return of Anamashta's heir, the Prophecy I had to fulfil with powers I still did not understand. Nearer to me was a curtain of flowers cascading down like a waterfall, a view only afforded by plentiful sources of it. The noise from the city was softened by the high walls, replaced by birdsong and the steady hum of pond insects. If you had never left these circles, you could believe that this was all there was to the world; but beyond the walls, the rest of Tabashi beckoned, poised to celebrate with lungs full of air and hearts brimming with song—for the centuries they had had to make do without.

How could I come to know both worlds and live—torn between them? I watched as people gathered around a moat encircling a magnificent stone pillar etched with depictions of the Great War: Wardhani atop an elephant, standing with soldiers locked in fierce combat with untamed jungle creatures. The peak spiralled upward, joined by soaring spires piercing the sky all across the cityscape, each crowned with dips and wells resembling stacked corn basking in the sun. Multi-headed nagas and a dual-trunked kunchuwarri adorned the antefixes of each building's roof, pursued by frolicking kikiriki. Our history was carved into every surface of the kingdom, taught in every school, and etched into every manuscript. What did it mean to be part of that? How does one even begin? Did Wardhani know they would carve her into the stone as she sacrificed herself on it? I observed a group of fishers depart from the harbour, their sampans bobbing in the crystal-clear waters of the bay. I thought of the *Bayanihan*; a part of me longed to be back out there with the familiar faces of the crew—Kato and Yuna, their laughter far from polite, and our meals far from luxurious, but its own sort of plenty.

I leaned against the balustrade, letting the breeze from the distant ocean cool the sweat that had already formed—nervous exertion from my spectacular performance as anything but what I am. I shut my eyes to recall the feel of it so strongly against my face, a feeling like flying, and breathed it in deeply. I reminded myself to be grateful, that there had been a time when this was the fantasy: a full belly, safe walls, and a title. I lingered there for as long as I could, observing the ebb and flow of life as it unfolded before me, until my gaze wandered from the scene and collided with that of a young woman standing at the balustrade, just a few paces away—the same maiden who had dressed me in my room. Bathed in the light, I could finally discern the fragile features of her face, an uncanny resemblance to a girl I had once known, a girl whose name I refused to let rest.

We were suspended in time, our stares fixed on each other, tethered to the invisible threads of a school that had burnt down with our names. How long had she been standing there? Did she mean to speak to me? Then, without another word, she pivoted and ran.

"Wait!" I cried out, my voice reaching for her as she vanished around a corner.

They think we can just be bought? I heard from the Council. As my heart raced, so too would the water to find me.

"Petakai would be nothing without our ships!" another countered. I tried to keep my breaths steady and my mind in the present as the Council's words continued to fly back and forth between my ears. "First our Exorci, now they want the entire kingdom too?"

"Who is this prince?" someone demanded.

"Who is the Estari?" another chimed in.

"How did she defeat the beast?" a third voice questioned.

Waves of the sea, a giant ship, council meetings in expensive halls, the day I had faced the naga, its serpentine body rising out of the water and crashing into my cheek—everything came in flashes. Rimi's cries, Nalini's eyes, the stowaway's blade. I sprinted down the winding corridors, feeling the cool air rush past me, keeping me there in what was real as I dodged past servants and guards. But I felt like I was chasing a ghost; I could only ever see her from the corner of my eye, whipping around to greet an empty corridor. The longer I searched, the more tested was my connection to the world. I was fighting to not let go for fear that without all the pieces, the entire picture would be forfeit. *Lahela Tabashi. I am—*

"Can she bring back the water?"

The voices broke against my back as I raced to outrun them, as if they weren't already a part of the doubt that pulled me under, the drought that had plagued our kingdom for centuries, the unrest stirring in our people in its wake. Could I really be part of their salvation? I knew that if the Council played their cards right, they could use my image as a tool, that the people would look to me as their saviour and a beacon of hope to light the way. The new alliance between Tabashi and Petakai would make us Great again. But the Council were the ones with their hands on the quill, drawing the borders between our lands and giving a reason for their divide, deciding where and how much and to whom we all would answer, and they intended to keep it that way. Still, I hoped—like one does when standing in a pit of vipers and someone throws down a thorny vine; you grit your teeth and you climb.

"There are more pressing matters," Rimi said. I turned to her, surprised to hear her in the sea. "If Lahela is to destroy the naga, she needs to strengthen her powers."

Rimi was right, and she understood my powers the most.

"So she's no use to us like this," Seriatha cooed, her judgement chilling. There was nothing for me to say or do, and they were probably tired of seeing me feign gratitude for their apparent kindness, wincing as every thorn dug into my palm in my attempt to climb. That's why I was no longer summoned. There was at least some truth to their words. If I was to fulfil the Prophecy and save Tabashi from its drought, I would need to be stronger, more powerful, and with the knowledge of how to wield that power.

"We can't help her here," a council member said at last, his voice heavy with resignation. "There is only one who can."

* * *

Lahela Tabashi. I am Lahela Tabashi, and I am running to catch my past.

I had rounded yet another corner of the palace in my chase when my heart leapt into my throat; the waves receded and there she stood, poised on a balcony overlooking the sprawling city below it. There were only a finite number of hiding places within these halls, where prying eyes seemed to scrutinise from every angle, and she'd finally stopped running from those determined to remember her. Draped in a wash of colour that made it seem like she had floated, a wisp of smoke, out of my dreams and into my waking state. With measured steps, I approached her.

"The city is so different from up here," she whispered solemnly, her gaze to the horizon. Memories surged within me; the last time we had both gazed upon this city was from the dusty courtyard of a humble boarding house, nestled in the valley and encircled by dying fields. I allowed her name to fill my thoughts, and with it came a downpour of our time at the Eyrell—playing simple games with wooden chips, makeshift pieces fashioned from scraps we'd scavenged, unlike the finely carved, oiled, and polished ones we knew now; eating sticky rice served on banana leaf plates shared with rowdy and weary children after the days spent weaving and sewing garments not unlike the ones we were wearing in the palace. My fingers traced the embroidery of my outfit, feeling in them the familiar sting of a wayward needle manoeuvred too quickly through the fabric.

"I'm glad you're here—Linh," I whispered, meaning an apology—coming out as a plea.

"Please don't speak to me," she said, meaning an apology—coming out as a warning. "I don't want them to know. I don't want their questions." Then she turned abruptly and left. The girl they had taken away in the royal carriage, believing her to be magical. We had all been so confused; she'd shown no signs of magic, but someone had purposefully misled them, for the real Exorci was still in hiding. How little we had had, but how much we had all lost. It was at that moment that Rimi came back to join me; I could tell from the sound of her footsteps before I even caught sight of her robe. I thought I'd have with my friend a reprieve from the tense encounter with Linh, but her expression was so severe I nearly stumbled backward from the force.

"Lahela," she fired, with a distinct edge.

"Is something wrong?" I asked, surprised.

"Why should something be wrong?"

"What did they—" I began, but she spoke ahead.

"Here we are gorging ourselves on fruit handed to us by elephants when we should be out there training—"

"For what?"

"The naga! What happens when they send you back out on a ship?"

"I—"

"Fancy clothes won't do you any good when you're fighting for your life."

"Rimisin, where is this coming from?" I demanded, but she'd turned from me. "Rimi!" I called out after her again, but she too was gone. Standing there alone, feeling very out of place and much too small for the dress that I was in, I ran my hands over the fabric and found a stray thread poking out from the embroidery—a mistake that would have cost us a meal back at the Eyrell. I pulled and watched as the beautiful swirling patterns unravelled before me.

* * *

"There is only one who can."

I remained silent as the voices grew, my gaze fixed on the patterned gold thread woven into the textile beneath the Council's feet; having stared at them for so long, I could have sworn they'd started swimming in the firelight. The shadows in the halls had grown bolder, shifting from smoke to inky tendrils stretching towards us. The night outside was as dark as a mountain beneath the waves.

"Hand her to the Bashantu? Are you mad?"

Reader, that was their plan. So that I could become the Estari they needed me to be, they were sending me straight into the mouth of the naga so that I could learn the strength of its bite. Then if, by chance, my powers saved me, they could pull me back out of the corpse and claim all the glory—at no expense to them. What was another girl with no title?

"The Bashantu hide the only known Estari in the kingdom."

It seemed village gossip reached even the high walls of the palace, and the talk that there was another Estari in the kingdom, and that the Bashantu was hiding them, was the most shocking of all. What kind of Prophecy did we have? We had already fulfilled it, and the one better equipped for the challenge refused the call. Reader, this was all news to me too, but the Council did not speak to me as if I had to know.

"That's just a rumour. You might as well believe Moultisjka leads the Bashantu."

Despite my wounds, I climbed the vine—hopeful for a ledge, anything to rest my weary arms and legs that had been tirelessly running since the moment I could animate them, so close now to some kind of respite. I couldn't go back down, not back towards the blood-red serpents, my throat staring down the blade of a machete. But what if the climb to salvation would kill me before I ever reached the top?

"The Estari is not a rumour, and we have no hope without them."

Silence, like a warning.

"How do we know they won't keep her too?"

Silence, like a decision.

Then at last, Seriatha spoke, her voice a serpent's hiss as I peered down from the vine. I had almost reached the summit, thorns snagging and tearing at my dress, my hands drawing blood.

"They won't," she said. The vine severed, and I plummeted.

✳︎ ✳︎ 24 ✳︎ ✳︎

The afternoon swirled by in a blur—eating and drinking, laughing at jokes I didn't understand, and mingling with guests I didn't know. After the charade, I could finally return to the quiet embrace of a bedroom that wasn't mine. The moment the doors to the room shut behind me, I collapsed, water poured out of me as if making room for the breaths I was taking after having drowned. I longed to be back on my modest woven mat, in our cramped room at the Eyrell, shared with all the other children; at least we had each other. Why could I only appreciate it properly once I had grown, looking back with fondness rather than living through the sting of the straw broom? I knew it was wrong to find my way back there, to romance the times of hardship; but I couldn't remain here, not if I wanted to remain at all.

Before the meeting I at least had a friend, and some allies; Rimi's dismissal had thrown me so far out that I was now struggling for air, every heave a reminder of how ill-equipped I was to appreciate the finery, how little I deserved it, how little they really meant it for me. *I am . . .* Who was I? Who was I without someone to say my name back to me? I couldn't even remember theirs, battered by the tide and lost in the swell. But in every way the water flowed, one stream stayed true to its course: the peace I would find in the dirt, my body a root to Shi. I clawed across the floor of my bedroom with the only strength I had left, climbing out of the window and finally into the garden. Sinking into the dirt, the setting sun wrapping its arms around my shaking body, the currents finally slowed their demand.

Those gardens were sublime—an entrance of deep-green vines winding their way around a towering sandstone pillar, curling leaves of a lotus flower carved into the base of the column. The humming of insects and the smell of damp earth on the breeze. I could have spent all my time there if allowed, just watching the way the wind caught on the leaves, rustling them; it was as if they were waving back. I imagined the trees whispering secrets about us. How many years had they known us, and in those years, how many secrets had they carefully kept?

My breaths settled, so I released myself from the ground; now was not the time for self-pity. Old habits die hard, and I wanted to give myself another choice where others would not; so, of course, I had to prepare. If I'd stayed there long enough in the garden, let my eyes adjust to the greenery, I might have glimpsed something small and round shining in the dirt, something dropped and forgotten. I might have retrieved it. I might have found and kept many shiny things, tucking them into the undergarment wrapped around my chest. Rounding the corners of that large but private enclosure, I thought of nothing else but collecting the colours of the dying light.

* * *

"I can't believe you!" I heard from behind some of the banana trees, momentarily distracting me from my quest for coins. Was that Nalini? Who could she have been speaking to? Despite my excitement at hearing a familiar voice, I flattened myself against a hedge in case my presence would not be welcome in her secret conversation; I was not noble enough to leave.

"Don't start."

That was the captain's voice.

"Tanhchana Drasari—you're a monster." *Drasari?*

"Nalini, please—"

"How could you? To Nari's child?" Nalini said. They must have been arguing about Rimi. Nari being the name of her mother, the woman they had all known, long before they lost her to the seas. Tanh must have finally told Nalini, or maybe she'd figured it out. It made sense they called that name now; Rimi's mother should be there for this conversation. I should have left, but I had to know too.

"We were being attacked! People die at sea all the time," the captain said.

"Oh Nari . . ."

"She was there! I asked for her forgiveness."

"And Alewic's? He's your friend!" Nalini barked.

"He's your friend. They're *my* crew."

"Of course—a pirate."

That same insult. When did Tanh become a captain? If Drasari was her name, what of her title?

"I never asked to be part of your world, Nalini Singh."

"Wardhani would never—and she was ten times the captain you are." So that was why the captain hadn't let me call her by that title; she also carried a dead girl's name. I thought back to our meeting at the docks—it was like recognising like.

"Maybe you're right," the captain sighed. There was a tense silence. I thought that if I tried to sneak away then, there was no chance they wouldn't hear me. I held my breath. Finally, the captain spoke. "It's a dirty business, my love. I've sacrificed a lot more than that to keep you afloat." Her voice was barely above a whisper. She was so tender—despite Nalini's cruel insults. There was so much more to their story that I didn't understand.

"Don't you dare put this on me," Nalini shot back. My stomach curled over itself.

"You know there's nothing noble about your kind."

"And what's my kind?" Then it was quiet, but not because they'd stopped communicating. I guessed Tanh had made a gesture with her hands to inspire Nalini's response. "You're impossible."

"Can't change me," replied the captain.

"I should have known that Alewic had made a deal with you to get him out of Petakai."

"He doesn't know. Nalini, it was all Rimi's idea." That's right—the deal, between Rimi and the captain, the one she made to board the *Bayanihan*.

"She's a child!" Nalini flared.

"She's smarter than you think," the captain finished. Then, after some time, she said, "She reminds me of you."

"You think that's a good thing to say to me right now?"

"I don't—I don't think, Nalini. Okay? I just do. Whatever I have to—for you."

"Then don't. We're done." I heard the shuffling of Nalini's garments as she left. I gathered my insides and turned to leave too, when I was suddenly stopped in my tracks.

"Satisfied?" the captain asked, facing me, having appeared from around the corner. I had to swallow a yelp.

"Captain," I said—feigning innocence.

"You need to work on your breathing."

"What?"

"In as they talk, hold while they think, release as they go again." I braced myself for the wave but never felt the crash. Eventually I realised: she'd known I was there, listening to their conversation, and she'd already forgiven me. I bowed my head to gesture my thanks

"Where will you go now?" I asked.

"Back to the ship," she replied easily.

"And what about Nalini?"

"She'll find me when she needs me."

"But—"

"This isn't the first time I've upset her, kid. We'll be alright," she assured me, resting a hand on my shoulder. "You look after yourself now."

Reader, I hugged her. It shocked us both, but eventually she hugged me back. "It's a thankless job, what you do," I mumbled into her shoulder. I was holding back tears.

"Well, someone has to," she joked.

"Thank you, Captain Tanhchana Drasari," I said with certainty. We lingered in our embrace long enough for it to become uncomfortable, the evening breeze a sharp reminder of where we were and what we had to do.

"Lahela," she said, gently grabbing me by the shoulders and holding me back to look into my eyes, "know who you are and decide what you do; that's all we've got to work with." She winked, then left. That was the first time she'd used my name to address me; it was the only thing holding me together. If she hadn't done it, I might have disappeared straight into the ground. Reader, every time someone calls you by a name, they let your spirit know its tether. I had spent so long without mine, it was time I came back into myself and to find out what it meant.

Lahela Tabashi. I am Lahela Tabashi. I belong to Tabashi— and I will fight for it.

* * *

I was climbing through the window back into my room when I locked eyes with Linh; she had also just entered, but from a door. Yet rather than scold, her lips curled upward. She waved me in and rushed over to the dresser to retrieve a new dress; I had ruined mine in the grass. These sorts of antics were familiar to the both of us; the heartache was not. I had kept my promise not to speak to her, as much as it pained me. I wondered why she was still my maiden, but perhaps it would have brought on more unwanted questions if she'd raised the issue at all; there was no reason for her not to be as far as the Council were aware. I wondered what name she used instead of Linh, whether she had chosen one, or whether they had given her one when they took her from us.

Linh made quick work of the outfit; it was a masterpiece: a metal framework of gold shaped to resemble the feathers of a kikiriki was fixed on my head, and caressing my form was a silk sash the colour of daylight above the sea, embellished with jewels that looked like silver fish in the river; the fabric cascaded down like the current. Golden earrings, shaped to elongate my own, to inspire ideas of Greatness, were added too, with an enormous jewelled necklace across my collarbone. It was awfully heavy, the ensemble, and I willed it to weigh down my wandering mind.

I traced my fingertips along the cool silk, wondering what the point was of all this luxury if there wasn't someone here to give it meaning. You can sometimes grow up and get the things you've always wanted only to realise you had lost what you had, and perhaps you wanted that more. I thought of a memory long washed away: her broad shoulders, knowing stance, and athletic prowess. She was a fighter, and an excellent one at that, built to rule, while I was built to hold her crown for her. But the tide decides what's left behind on the sand; if I held on too long she would slowly slip through my fingers, becoming one with the water. So I released her memory back into the sea, accepting that all I could do was hope for its gentle return.

Thank you, I mouthed graciously to Linh as she turned to beckon me through the doors.

* * *

The halls of the palace had exploded in a blaze of colour and splendour. Hundreds of guests were illuminated in the glow, awash with the colours of the setting sun. Feathered headdresses, glittering shawls, and vividly painted faces decorated the assembly. Some guests carried tiny monkeys on the end of leashes. I thought of Tanh, of the many leashes she would sever with her blade; would she face this crowd with courage or dread?

Their voices melded together, a harmonious chorus, their laughter twinkling like the walls basked in candlelight. I listened intently, searching for a familiar melody, the voice of a girl I'd travelled across the ocean with only to find ourselves parted at the shore. A sudden clap of thunder reverberated through the hall, followed by a burst of colour that splashed against the floor—fireworks. Amidst the throng I spotted my silver fish; a flash of Rimi's signature blue braid. Relief washed over me; I envisioned Alewic charming the crowd with his whimsical displays, and there she would be too—beaming. I was desperate to find her, for a chance to speak. What had they said to her? Why was she so upset with me? I needed assurance that we were on the same side, that I still knew my friend.

I hoped to pass through the crowd unnoticed. Yet, like the *Bayanihan* cleaving through the waves, the sea of gold and glitter parted before me, casting a cascade of unwanted attention in my direction. Every creature in the room knew who I was; the matrix of metal on my ears and collarbone and the colour of my robes announced my status—even when my temperament could not. I shifted within my elaborate disguise, feeling like an imposter amongst the elite. Each one of them had their own version of the tale, and thus their own judgments of the character. Melded to the ground by the heat of their stares and unable to continue my search, I came to accept that there was not a single blue braid in sight; Rimi must have vanished, alerted to my arrival by the grandiosity of it, supported by an orchestra of wide-eyed inquisition.

I felt like I was in a clear pond, the royal herons circling—peering into my depths beneath the unforgiving light of day. Any moment now someone would lunge at me for the water, seeking solace from their unquenchable thirst, and who could fault them? In this land? In this century? But another force soon demanded their attention: the approach of Seriatha Navindi. She parted the sea not by spectacle, though she was terrifyingly breathtaking, but with the sheer force of her presence. The Council had limited my interactions with her, experiencing them as lashes from the other end of the meeting room, but now she strode directly towards me with a burning focus, enough to sear all water in the pond, leaving everyone else without. I attempted a respectful bow, but I think I betrayed my unease.

"You're late," she hissed, her scorn unmistakable. Then, just as quickly as she'd appeared, she moved on. Those were the first words spoken to me that evening; I was left to endure the curious stares from those who'd witnessed them. But the pond was barren, save for the decorative flowers quickly drying up in the heat. Thus, without a friend at my side, I joined the procession of guests into the dining hall.

*   *   *

Aromas of sweet sticky rice, deep-fried fish, lemongrass, and lime wafted out to greet us; it was a warm welcome, well before we could behold the magnificent spread ourselves. This was a special occasion after all, the Festival of Gathering, and the return of the rain. I wore Anamashta's colours—they had done that on purpose—and bore her visage as if she'd stepped out of one of the murals that lined the walls. Though I doubted that in the flesh the woman could have always dressed so resplendently, given that she was busy with an entire kingdom to replenish.

I could not let my sullen mood dampen my curiosity for the feast; it would be a shame to let any of the delicious food, or my privileged opportunity to graze it, go to waste. I was grateful for the chatter, for it masked the inevitable grumble of my belly. The haunting melody of a khene soon joined the chorus; music from bamboo pipes, bound by hardened sap, transported us to a bygone era when lands thrived with verdant fields and fish-filled rivers. If only the walls could animate and we could dwell in them, finally at peace. I have always known the dying land and the scorching sky; I wondered if I really could save them all, myself included.

Suddenly, from the very edges of my vision, I saw a flash of red. I spun with such force that the metal framework almost toppled over, and I had to reach my hands up just to steady it. *Was that real? Lahela Tabashi, I am Lahela . . .* I was quickly ushered over towards the Council at the head of the banquet hall and motioned to sit cross-legged on a soft fringed cushion at one of the low tables, surrounded by chattering voices and the clinking of metal. I fiddled with the fringe as the other guests joined me at my table. Though we were still welcome to eat with our hands, I was sitting amongst those with an education for the finer way to dine. I swallowed my nerves and tried to blend in, watching as the others brought mounds of food loaded onto delicate silverware to their lips and attempting to do the same—with varying degrees of success.

"The wine is strong indeed!" I heard from across the table. I cowered behind a crimson tide. All the guests were seated facing their own conversation, and we were all on a level lower than the Council. There was a visible distinction between outfits from the crowd that had gathered in the streets to the ones that dined in the royal banquet halls. Now the robes were finer, the colours more vivid, and the embroidery exceptionally detailed. On the wealthiest of guests were layers of belts and cuffs adorned with emeralds and sapphires; but none were as extravagant as the headdresses and jewellery on the Council, or their prophesied heir.

Before us on the table was steaming sticky rice, perfectly tender and fragrant, nestled beside freshly caught river fish, their scales glinting like gems, next to curries and spices and an orchestra of sweet fruits, rich mango and coconut desserts to finish. The hall filled with delighted chatter, of guests intoxicated by rice wine that had been aged to perfection. Children had grasped fish heads in their tiny hands, mimicking speech and laughter with their puppets' jaws, their faces filled with mischief. The air was a blend of warm incense and perfumed diners, brightened with the fresh citrus on the table. The smoke wrapped itself around our spirits, lifted ever higher as the night wore on by the flames lighting the halls. I could have flown too, if only I weren't so bound by the weight of my costume.

I tried one more time to find a face I would recognise in the unyielding sea of colourful strangers and their maniacal glee but resigned myself to a feeling of solitude despite the busy congregation. I ate quietly, adrift in a sea of my own. Food was always a comfort, but even the bounty before me was eventually eclipsed by the murmurs that creeped in beside me. Furtive glances cast my way. Tendrils of whispers snaking their way around my wrists and collarbone. Attempting to be passive, I ignored them and thought I might again find solace beneath the surface. Until, with a gentle grace, a presence emerged beside me that enticed me to linger—Nalini, dressed in a striking blue gown, shimmering with each step she took, like the ocean curling beneath the moonlight. She looked incredible, as she always did.

"May I join you?" she asked, offering a friendly smile; it had been some time since I had seen one of those. I nodded, a little giddy and still stunned by her sudden appearance.

"Excellent. Perhaps tonight won't be dreadfully boring after all," she said, before helping herself down. I let out a quiet chuckle, the sensation loosening the invisible ties around my chest and lifting the weight of the jewels. This was the friendliest she'd ever been to me—I definitely couldn't tell her I'd overheard her in the garden. I wondered if she was also masking her feelings, having come here alone.

Nalini took the seat next to me and ate with her hands, making small talk about the food and the decorations. Her voice was so soothing, her manner so familiar, I finally relaxed in the company of someone I knew and who had spent some time getting to know me. I quickly abandoned my humorous attempt at using cutlery to join her in the fun. We never spoke about anything that mattered, but it was enough to just have her there. As the meal approached its end, the room dimmed with the extinguishing of candles and the guests fell silent in response. All gazes converged on a single warm light at one end of the hall, casting its glow upon a plain expanse. As if on cue, a resonant voice filled the air.

"A long time ago, before we needed walls, the people and the beasts of the Jungle would live together in harmony." A shadow appeared on the expanse. Detailed cuttings in a piece of painted buffalo hide, it depicted the image of a jungle beast, an animal with the body of a tiger but the head of a naga, with scales and fur alike. Then another shadow appeared on the opposite side, the shadow of a person trying to tame it. The story was told like this, an intricate dance of light and colour to reveal the origins of our times, Shi's magic, the Great War, and our never-ending struggle with the Jungle. The creatures had once helped us to shape our lands, creating the rivers and channels that brought water from the mountains in the north to flood the rice fields below, then out into the ocean when the land was ready to welcome the dry season at last—a balancing of the times of plenty with a chance to earn it through toil. Back then, every being understood that balance, taking only what they could give back in kind. But one day someone born with great magical ability, but a great lust for power, used magic to destroy the way things were, to make room for the way they thought it should be. A menacing voice of warning called out her name and even the eldest in the halls, familiar with the tale, quietened to make room for it.

"Moultisjka the Terrible."

"But now we celebrate a new age," Seriatha pronounced. The entire hall turned to welcome her voice from her seat at the highest table. "An age of abundance and prosperity. The return of the rain. The return of—"

"Not by blood."

A collected gasp. From the other end of the hall, as clear as lightning cutting through a stormy sky, a woman covered head to toe in red, having stood in the gathering silence, made herself known. I knew I'd seen it; the colour was unmistakable—she was real. But I recognised her only from the colour of her dress and not by the features of her face. The stowaway was still nowhere to be seen, if she was even near the palace. I had to catch myself—realising I'd been wondering, *What was she doing in my blue?*

"They come here claiming Anamashta's heir just as they claimed their seats of power when we lost our king," she began, and I wished to sink into the floorboards—watching as all heads flickered back and forth between us. Seriatha's own eyes darkened with a terrible storm.

"They parade their false prophet while we starve! Not my blood!" the red woman spat, pointing her chin—and the accusations of her rallying cry—towards the Council. I heard the whispers, felt their searing stares, but there was nothing left for them to burn. The Council motioned for the guards and they made for the red woman through the crowd.

"How long since these lands flourished? How long since our ancestors crossed the seas?" she cried out, un-moving and unfazed. The guards would fall upon her like a landslide and she would stand there for as long as her foundations could withstand them, continuing her fight.

"How long since they cut us off from those who might help us? The ocean became dangerous because of their corrupted magic!" she was screaming, as arms surged to blanket her in layers of glittering gold and metal, piling on top of her and silencing her under the weight of authority. I heard the gasps, the shocked faces of the guests; people who had come here from all parts of Tabashi and beyond to hear some good news—finally.

"I don't want news of a new age," a man stood up, clad in blue with a headdress of silver and a small bird on his shoulder—a baby kikiriki with a golden beak. "I want to go home to Petakai," he said, and as he finished, his bird cawed. Something moved between the people then, something greater than the Council could control—a gathering storm. The guards fanned out, ready to catch the fires, but the wind had gotten to them first, and rather than blow them out, I watched them climb the tapestries, setting them ablaze.

"They cursed the path through the Jungle to my home—to Lenfol!" another banquet guest rose to their feet, their voice trembling with emotion. The kingdom to the north; tales of a war smouldering beneath an impenetrable border, old alliances forged in the fires of necessity; people who had journeyed here to begin anew only to find their loyalties tested as a kingdom's famine eclipsed its desires for conquest. "No more false idols and hollow claims to the throne. No more deception!"

"Restore my home!" came a voice from someone seated at my table. "Tabashi thrived before your people trespassed our borders. Leave—and take the monsters with you!"

The instigator of the unrest, having nearly crossed the threshold of the palace entrance, found herself restrained by guards who now faced a new surge of maddened palace guests drunk on perfectly aged rice wine. A devious smile graced the red woman's face as she offered little resistance, her intentions laid bare.

"We should leave," Nalini said quickly. She grasped my wrist, lifting me to my feet before my legs could obey the command.

"My family has tended this land since Shi's creation. They die for it! The Council mock us behind their opulence—I refuse to bow to heretics! Not by blood! Not my blood!" someone else called out. I couldn't see their faces.

"Not by blood! Not my blood!" the crowd repeated. The fire roared and the flames gathered to collide with each other—a skirmish between people, lands, and kingdoms. Guards swiftly guided the Council to safety down hidden walkways, and Nalini and I followed close behind. More guards swarmed past us, returning to the banquet hall.

"Shut the doors!" Seriatha demanded, but the unstoppable force pressed on. They led us through serpentine corridors that darkened with each step, until, at last, we emerged into the cool embrace of an open courtyard at the back of the palace, bordering the Jungle. I frantically searched for Rimi amongst the throng of concerned nobility and their personal guards but I couldn't make her out from the other hooded soldiers. Nalini released my wrist, and the fleeting calm she had provided evaporated with the blaze.

"Wait here," she instructed and made her way back towards the people with answers.

✶✶ 25 ✶✶

Away from the noise and under the wide night sky, I let out a resounding breath and gazed up at the stars. For once, they seemed to smile back at me. Despite it all, I noticed how easily my breath came, how quickly the rapids had dislodged the stones. Though I was at their mercy, I knew in my heart that water always had to flow from one place to another; even the rice fields needed floods for the crop to grow, and there is nothing more dangerous than a sitting pond. There was truth in those halls, finally. I could feel my heart beating in my chest, and the blood that pooled there—*it was real.*

I breathed in slowly, my bare feet on the damp grass. I welcomed the night, seeking solace in the sounds of the creatures of the Jungle, drawn to its mountainous expanse beyond the walls, the rainforest cascading from its heights, bathing in the evening's light. The trees glowed, creating an illusion of a waterfall spiralling down the hill. I glanced back at the palace, realising none observed me; their focus lay on the halls' disquiet. So I hiked up my garment, hearing the clinking of the heavy jewels clinging to my frame, and made my way through the darkness, away from the distracting light of the candles and further into my mind. I heard something, or felt something, in the dreamlike sea—the one I'd called to me with my eyes shut. I could sense it ahead, powerful and with an intent, moving like the naga beneath the waves. Looking out at the garden, I found it tranquil and sublime, the only sound coming from the crickets and the distant calls of the guests still demanding justice; their shouts faded into a fountain ahead. I made my way over towards it and peered into the pond at its feet. The fountain was carved into the shape of a blooming lotus, with its leaves climbing up the stone support behind it. The scene was inviting, so I waded into the water.

It felt cool and soft against my skin as I slowly found my footing. I could reach the bottom of the pond with only half of my calf beneath the surface, but I had to hike up my garment further to keep it from getting wet. This far away from the crowd and with only the trickling in my ears, I let my senses envelop me. I heard the quiet buzzing of the insects and felt their gentle vibrations on the surface. As I approached the centre of the pool, the thing that I had sensed beneath the surface took form; it was too large to be a fish but too agile to be anything else. It moved with a sense of purpose, searching for something. As I stood there, I could feel the currents changing around me. I noticed the moonlight rippling on the surface—I realised I had seen this reflection before; that light had not come from the moon.

Reader, I am going to share a memory that has taken me this long to unveil. Sometimes I wish to stretch out every moment I had with her, and sometimes it's all too much. I would keep it to myself—indefinitely, if I could, fighting for it like a village girl holding onto her last wooden chip. But you must understand, I discovered the water long ago. The challenge lies in accepting that all rivers, in their ceaseless flow, will always lead me back to this. I wrote the tale in earnest, so I too must brave the currents.

* * *

We had finally executed our plan to escape the Eyrell. We knew we would head towards the trees and hide in their shade. Shadowing the road, following it towards the city, but then turning towards Kern. From there, we could find a new life together, perhaps even travel north one day, all the way to Lenfol and into a new life. Across the dirt, we ran, our destination almost within reach. The Jungle loomed, visible as a stain blacker than the night against the backdrop of the evening. We crashed through the brush, scraping our knees. But something else moved against the light of the moon, catching it in a shimmer that broke the surface of a small channel of water not too far from us. So we halted, breaths caught in our throats, torn between the desire to blend into the darkness and a curiosity too potent for children to ignore. Drawn to the source of the reflection, we found a brilliant secret hidden beneath a banana leaf. She jumped into the water first, the silver light darting from her.

"It's a fish!" she shrieked, and for a moment we completely forgot about our plans of escape—such are the whims of children, wild minds easily carried off by the dangerous night. We raced to keep up with the skittering moonlight, climbing the damp and struggling to find our footing as the leaves broke apart beneath us. I saw the creature leap out of a pond and onto a stone, carrying itself on four legs before diving back into a small waterfall.

"It's not a fish!" I cried back. It was a small white cat, I swore it, with blue and silver stripes that glowed in the water, trailing a long tail with webbed fins. It was then that I leapt into the water too, unable to help myself. We were in the Jungle, too excited to be afraid, but the mud was slowing me down.

"It's okay," I said, low and quiet into the night, wading my way through the shadows. I felt drawn to something when, from under a wide palm leaf, two ears pricked the crisp night air above the pond, then a pair of eyes, followed by the pale tip of a purple nose.

"There it is!" she whispered harshly from behind me. Again, I shushed her.

"Don't be frightened. We will not hurt you," I said to a timid face coming into view. "Are you the moon?" I asked.

"It looks like a tiger," she exclaimed, making her way over to crouch down beside me, frightening the creature back into invisibility.

"It's okay. She's a friend," I said into the water. It was silent for a while, too long for wild minds.

"Let's go," she said suddenly and went to help me up. But then—

"There it is!" I exclaimed, as the creature appeared once more in a rippling light.

"What . . . is it?" we both asked. We could finally see it in its full brilliance. Out from the water rose a wet nose followed by the wide and soft face of a white baby tiger, with silver iridescent stripes that seemed to drip and flow back into the stream it stepped out of. Two tiny glowing silver horns jutted out from its forehead, with eyes that glowed to match its body in the clear blue.

"It's . . . a water tiger? Is that right, creature?" I asked with the respect that it was due. It shook its damp fur in response and came closer. I reached an eager hand out to it and it sniffed me, carefully nudging the tips of my fingers, not unlike many of the village cats I'd been kind to, offering them dried fish. Just like with them, but without a fish to offer, I gave the tiny white tiger a scratch behind its ears.

"It likes you!" she exclaimed.

"What do we name it?" I asked.

"You can't name a water tiger, Lahe." *Lahe*, that was what she used to call me; no one else ever has. The sound caressed my cheek. This memory belonged to that name, and that name to her.

"Why not?" I challenged.

"Because it doesn't belong to you. It belongs to the Jungle."

"But I know this one," I said with a pout. "What do I name my memories then? Those belong to me, don't they?" I asked. This gave her pause, and we both searched for the answer. I looked back up at the moon in the sky, then back down at the one in the water in front of me. "What about 'Chandra'?"

"That's not a word," she said cleverly. I poked my tongue out at her.

"It's a name. For my memories of the moon." I shook a few droplets off my hand, and Chandra shook too. It caused us both to giggle. "My friend, Chandra."

"Hi, Chandra," she said.

"I'm Lahela, and this is—"

Reader, I am still not ready to give this up. You will receive her name in the same blow that was dealt to me, after all those many years.

"—and this is how we will remember each other."

* * *

Tigers are truly sacred creatures. We revere them as guardians of the Jungle, and also as one of its many terrible beasts. While we often seek certainty, ultimate truths, the tigers remind us that those are as fluid as water. They are both danger and protector, an omen of great power to come, but one earned through great sacrifice. Remember that everything comes back to the balance of things—a gift for a curse. What would you sacrifice to relive a sweet memory? What would you give to bring back the rain?

Emerging from the lotus pond that I was still standing in, my memories of the creature receded into the real one—the wet purple nose of a white tiger as it surfaced from the water. It had an expansive gentle face like the sculptures that guarded the palace entrance, with silver iridescent stripes along its back, blending seamlessly back into the pond, and a pair of silver horns to match. I had to step back to make room for the rising creature and quickly understood why it had not fully materialised in the water; its adult body was far too large for the vessel it had poured out of.

"Chandra," I whispered into a familiar haze, calling the moon to me; its colossal paw broke the water's surface, touching the soft grass before being joined by another. These mighty limbs supported the giant form of a jungle tiger rising out of the water, locking its gaze with me. Droplets raced down its body to rejoin it in the pond, while others melded with its fur—now materialising. I bowed, our tether unbroken from the past, twin moons surrendering to the tide.

"There, in the pond!" someone yelled behind me. Panic seized me like a vine as I remembered. I turned to face them, just as Chandra let out a ferocious snarl, half of it resting on the grass while the rest of it remained submerged in the pond.

"*A beast!*" I heard from ahead of me, and in a memory. My mind shattered, as did my heart; in two places, across two timelines, the twin rivers came to a head. I braced myself for the rapids, my body collapsing onto the dirt with my arms as supports, my knees in the pond.

* * *

We heard our names called out against the symphony of the night; we had missed our window of escape. Chandra dissolved back into the water. Panic gripped us.

"They're going to catch us!" she cried out, helping me up from the mud. "Hurry!" she urged, but I was stuck.

"What about Chandra?" I gasped, tears blurring my senses.

"It'll find us in the Jungle!" she urged, as she reached her arms around me and pulled with all her might. "Lahe, come on!" But it was already too late.

"There they are!" came the voices as the glow of their lanterns blinded us. Grasping hands reached for our small bodies; her hand was ripped from mine. I flailed helplessly as she kicked and screamed, their arms around her and catching her clothes like brambles. We were only children; we were powerless to fight them. The rage I felt then still burned within me, as clear as day. I would not be so powerless now.

* * *

"Kill it!" I heard, as the Exorci's eyes glowed, unmistakable in their black uniform. A dark line of hooded figures, indistinguishable from each other, all crowned with Moultisjka's fiery gaze. My body reared in response to the sight. I was contorting myself like the wild creature behind me. Felt a surge like a tidal wave welling up behind the tears, and I raised my arms like I had that day on the ship. I had attempted nothing like it since, but the movement felt familiar and as natural as drawing breath. I found myself enveloped by the sea, its currents swirling around me like ribbons I could grasp with my bare hands. Time seemed to slow, and I drew the ribbons to myself, one by one, creating a vortex of my rage like a shield, like a typhoon; the storm intensified with my cries. Something that had once existed only at the periphery of my mind, controlled by a will to blend in and make peace, now erupted into the world, unleashing its full fury like a tempest. At the centre of the maelstrom, the insatiable anger of a child discovering a world that is not fair.

"Lahela!" I heard too late as I let it surge. The torrents I'd summoned blinded me. When we fought the naga, it was like I fell into a dream; the night's tides had carried me with it, plunging me into the abyss. Every time I tried to recall that night, I could only ever feel a shiver, an unfinished painting turned over too soon but demanding an image to form. But in that instance, I was wide awake. The power that I had only felt like a whisper calling from the furthest reaches of my dreams came crashing into me with the storm.

Reader, if the ocean's tides follow the moon in the sky, imagine what it looked like to have the moon right there behind me; imagine the call, and the crash. Before it hadn't felt like a choice—eyes shut and my body at the mercy of the currents. But in the waking fury that stirred me, my memories, a thundering of everything taken, torn apart by the hands of circumstance—by the hands used to play a game of counting that damned a kingdom. I felt in my body the first chance I'd ever had to make a real choice: do I quiet the storm, or do I welcome the rain?

Reader, oh how I surrendered. I'd never fallen so fast in my life.

✳︎ ✳︎ 26 ✳︎ ✳︎

Water breaks against a rock and crashes into itself, the bubbles frothing and churning away with the rapids, summoned by a name and pooling towards a face before it slices itself and shatters, the current unforgiving in its flight. In a way, all rivers lead to this, though I seldom understood that then. I reached for her and she reached back; I would grasp her this time.

"Lahela!"

Rimi's scream cut through the storm like a tear of lightning straight through my dark sky; it broke apart the memory and tore me from the torrent, a wave in complete opposition to the chaos, a mountainous swell that threatened to reverse the summoned typhoon. I saw in myself a girl who had spent her life running away, past all recognition, racing as fast as her little legs allowed to not let the past catch up with her and swallow her whole; a girl afraid to fall, head first, into an open sea, not because she didn't love the swell, but because she was afraid that no one would be there to pull her out again. But there she was, a friend, a beacon in the night whose light they could not diminish through thunder or ruin. Her eyes were wide and loving, her smile warm, and her hand reached out to find the girl through the storm. The softness of her edges blurred my vision, and I felt the currents of my anger rising to meet her calm, pushing back against it with an almighty force. The deep hurt, having waited for so long to be set free to unmake itself, would not go down without a fight.

But I reached back, with the small part of me that still yearned to be found, stretching an ever-so-steadying hand out from under an unbearably unsteady arm, and clasped my fingers around the only lifeline thrown to me. As my knuckles curled, I felt them burn. The fire, Reader, was unlike anything I remembered. Rimi's power glowed with a brightness I had never seen in her before, and the sensation of her hand in mine was like trying to grasp the tendrils of an unfurling blaze. Steam rose around us, mixing with the air and water and flames. I opened my mouth to scream, but the sound was gone, drowned out by the fire and thunder. We raged together against the tide, a deafening cascade of blaze burning the storm that tried to extinguish it.

"I know your pain!" Rimi howled at me, her voice rumbling with the typhoon. "I felt it the night I lost my mother. It rages inside you and you want so badly to let it out, to let it all escape so that you can stand there—safe in the eye of the storm." And she was right. Being there in the midst of the ocean's inferno, I felt the anger all around me and so was free from the way it burned inside, the way it thrashed at the body that tried to hold it, threatening to destroy the thing that sustained it. "Lahela, if you don't learn to contain it, to live with it, then you'll flood the entire world; then it's you out there alone, staring back at the sunken place you made."

"That *I* made! My place—for *me*!" I screamed. "Then I finally get a say in how I'm hurt!" I hurled back at her, the wind whipping around me, catching my words and throwing them into the fire.

"That's it then? You and the entire ocean? Is that the dream? Nothing but water between you and everything you once touched?" She reeled against the tide to match it with the same ferocity. Rimi had summoned something powerful enough to meet me in my maelstrom; she was showing me kindness, despite the darkest depths of my undoing. "I know you don't feel it now, but one day you will want to reach out to them; one day you will want to reach out beyond your rage to the people who have always been there reaching back. Please don't let them drown."

How far I had fallen into the dark. How far she had to reach for me. Reader, the quiet truth about fires—and the devastation they leave behind—is that deep down, they don't want to die.

* * *

Rimi's words echoed in my mind and I drifted on the breeze that wafted in with the haunting melody of a khene singing the songs of an age so familiar now it feels like a memory. I welcomed the profound stillness. Beyond the storm lay calmer seas, an open sky, and the body of a large ship bobbing peacefully on the tides. A crew was waving back: Kato, Yuna, and the face of a captain who fought for freedom. Nalini, her partner in justice, smiled down at me from the ship's bow. Alewic launched a firework into the cloudless night, illuminating the stars above. Rimi's laughter, genuine and unbridled by social propriety, was in harmony with the breeze. A feeling that I had been running away from, or perhaps chasing; lost, but not gone; fleeting, but not over. In the fight for your life, the only breath that matters is your last; breathe in, or let go? Breathe—I could, because they helped me, because I wanted to.

* * *

The tempest gradually subsided, in equal part, by Rimi and my undoing. The clouds receded towards the distant horizon, and the thunder that had deafened us gave way to the soothing murmur of gentle waves rocking back and forth against my eyelids. I felt the song finish, a resounding hum, and Rimi released my hand. The sensation struck like the aftermath of a storm, a final gust that stole the breath from my lungs. The consequences of my actions for what had transpired. A crushing realisation that I was very real, my feet on solid ground, and that the horrible things I had tried to do were real too.

I am Lahela Tabashi, and I had risked the safety of not only my life but also the lives of everyone within my reach. Thinking of Alewic, Nalini, and others who had spent the past few weeks fighting for a better deal in a game that was rigged from the start. Of them being harmed by my inability to control my powers or the emotions that fuelled them. The guilt was unbearable, but it was mine to carry if I wanted to make sure it would never hurt them. I raised my head to see the palace guards approaching, their expressions unwelcoming, but worst of all, marked with fear. One of them pointed a shaky finger at me, his voice was rough and quivering. "Was that all your magic?"

I turned to see that Chandra had vanished into the night, leaving behind a soft trickling fountain leading into a diminished and still pond, empty of life. To them, it must have seemed like I'd summoned Chandra, a beast of my creation—just like the storm, just like the women in the stories. How could I explain any of it? I barely understood it all myself. Even when logic and words finally found me again, I was speechless.

My royal garments were ruined, drenched in water and ragged from the wind as I stood helplessly trembling in the pond, the cool air of the night biting my skin. I looked to Rimi for answers, but I knew that if I reached for her mercy, I would only make her punishment worse. The Council would question her part in it all. I didn't know how much they understood of our magic, nor whether they knew she'd summoned her blaze to match my storm. But I had pulled her into the danger and she was just as much a part of the wreckage; we cannot extinguish our powers on our own. If Rimi had rallied a fire big enough to fight me and I hadn't sent water in equal amounts to put it out, we may not have been able to make it out together. I saw the pain in her face as she marched away from me to join the other Exorci.

I opened my mouth to answer, to tell them I meant no harm now and that I had made a mistake, but before I could utter a word, someone from the crowd screamed, "She's a witch! A danger!" I felt the fear in my heart, akin to what Rimi must have experienced her entire life. But it wasn't my fault—*was it?* In that moment I was both the young girl burned, standing scared and alone in the cold, and the woman who had to reason with her to come home to the hearth. I could not promise that it would never hurt again, only that we would try to figure this whole thing out together.

I focused on the crowd before me to discern the details of their faces. Their panic emerged; people were buckled over and spluttering on the grass, coughing up phlegm, while others were crying for them. Were they choking because they couldn't breathe? Had they been drowning? *Did I do that?*

"We could have died!" someone called out to me.

Somehow a few guests from the dining hall had found their way into the garden. Before me was more than the Council and the nobility; I saw the terrified faces of the citizens of Tabashi, people who had come here seeking a saviour only to be met with false hope, the stirring of a rebellion, and the threat of another mythical tyrant with unyielding powers. Our stories were so simple: Anamashta's water brought life, Moultisjka's fire—death. I looked down at my hands, their wrinkled lines and the shiver in them from the cold, so small for the devastation they could cause. I bet none of us expected that Anamashta's supposed heir could also carry the danger that Moultisjka's powers unleashed all those centuries ago. "Cursed Estari!" a voice called out, confirming my fears. "Curse them all!"

I had used my magic to protect Chandra, and myself, for all the times that I couldn't have before. *Hadn't I done the right thing?* Maybe it was the right thing, and time marches on, indifferent to sacrifice—unconcerned with regret. Are we defined by those moments? Forced to walk a path laid out by choices we had made when it had seemed like there were no others? Or are there simply many paths and we are the walking?

The guards closed in on me, and at that moment, I let them.

✼ ✼ 27 ✼ ✼

I waited in solitude, the dim candlelight casting long shadows around me as I stood outside the Council's meeting room, my focus waning and wandering to the painted walls. I looked for a distraction in the beings of our land, great and small: playful elephants and cheeky monkeys, birds in abundance of all different shades, and even the smallest geckos scurrying along on the dirt; all belonged, all were part of Tabashi, all descendants of Shi. How I longed to join them in the murals, to find myself in a land and time long lost but lingering like a name you can't quite place; you know it's real, but only as long as you try to remember it.

Within the Council, muffled voices and sharp tones forged my destiny with the heat of their arguments, debating whether I alone was to blame for the power unleashed, or if the beast was real and had caused the storm. They wondered if Rimisin had fuelled it further, and where the origins of my magic lay, whether I really could be Anamashta's heir. But no matter the path their discussion took, they agreed on a single point: that I was a threat to their way of doing things. I wondered if in being Tabashi's saviour, I would be the Council's undoing. The doors finally swung open, revealing a face so unfriendly I wished the truth of it had stayed closed to me.

"The events of today must never be repeated," Seriatha announced, her words directed at me but with a volume that would suggest an address to a crowded hall of protesters. I studied her features again. Each time we met, I unveiled a force of her might to be reckoned with. I was again faced with that reckoning. Imposing but slender, in the daylight she stood barely a foot taller than me, yet in her gown and shrouded in the night, she towered above me like the grand canopies of the borders at her command.

"Of course—" I began shakily.

"Tomorrow you shall accompany the royal procession to present gifts and convey goodwill to the villagers. You will repair the damage you caused," she said darkly.

"Are you disappointed?" I asked, wondering if maybe it would mean they would let me go.

"Quite the contrary, you're exactly what we've been waiting for," she replied, and my heart sank. I bowed as she dismissed me with a wave of her hand. I felt the urge to retreat to my quarters, tears poised at the edge of my vision. But before I could scurry away, I glimpsed Rimi exiting the room in Seriatha's wake, and I hurried to reach her. But when our faces met, her expression betrayed no hint of happiness at my approach.

"Rimi!" I called out, trailing her through the connecting corridors. "Rimi, what did they say?"

"They're going to send you out there because they know you'll be targeted," she revealed.

"By who?" I asked.

"The Bashantu," she said.

"What?"

"They'll kidnap you."

"That's absurd."

"Not if they dress you up as one of us." *Us?*

"Do you mean an Exorci?"

"It's who they target. They're building their own army by stealing ours," she replied.

"Ours?" I repeated angrily. But not at her.

"That day in the carriage, it wasn't you they were after. I should have known. I should have just let them take me and save the field," she said, cursing herself. So the ambush hadn't been about the Prophecy; it was a routine attack from the Bashantu. They were gathering Exorci, *for war?*

"How could you have known? None of this is your fault—" I began.

"They'll take you, then you'll spy on them. Learn from their Estari. When the time is right, the Council will unleash their attack on the Bashantu, as they've always planned to, and you'll be ready to help them win."

I was stunned. I thought that the Council barely had a handle on the situation, but it seemed like they'd been planning their advance this whole time; this was the war that they were preparing for, and with the arrival of my powers, they could finally set the plan in motion. How many wheels were already turning, and whose side was I really on? The world seemed to be ever expanding and I was stuck, so small in the face of it all, just trying to get back to my friend.

"How—" I began, but Rimisin forged ahead.

"They will station me nearby to keep watch," she said sharply—just like the Exorci in the mines, pulling people out from a collapsing tunnel to save them. But if she was there, then who would escort the crew across the sea? Then I realised: they were taking her away from the ocean, from her mother. That's what she'd been contending with all day, that's why she couldn't bear to face it, but she was a soldier, and she had her orders. I should have told her that I understood why she was upset; we should have talked about that. But instead, all I could think to say was, "And when were they going to tell me?"

"You'll perfect your powers, defeat their naga," she kept going; she was spiralling. Her tone was so cold; I responded to the chill rather than the hurt.

"It's all planned, is it? Your orders?" I hurled back.

"You'll marry the prince," she jeered.

"Do I at least get to know the day of my own wedding?" I snapped, and she finally stopped her maddening race down the hall. Rimisin spun around to confront me with the same intensity of our clash in the pond; we may have successfully contained the storms within the confines of our hearts, but there they would continue to burn.

"They won't need me on their ships anymore!" she blared.

"Just leave then! I don't understand—" I said, meaning an apology, coming out as apathy.

"Of course you don't understand! You never had to do this," she fired back.

"Do what exactly?" I said, my tone betraying my judgement of her character. It was finally out there in the open, a truth about us that would always be at odds.

"Sacrifice. For the good of the people."

"What?!" I yelled—incredulous—unable to keep our presence or our conversation hidden anymore. How could she make this about them? How could she not see the impact it had on me—the pressure, and my past? All sympathy evaporated. I was caught in the blaze of my fury. If we had been any less capable of holding ourselves together, our magic might have torn the hallways apart.

"And we make things work for you when you don't even want to be here," she spat, her voice burning. After everything we had endured—together. "Saviour of Tabashi, heir to the Great. Your powers are such a *gift*," she uttered, those last words filled with such contempt. That fight, the rapids that raged, it was about more than just me; the stones were finally dislodging. This fight was bigger than both of us; we were lashing out at a lifetime of injustices—an anger that was terribly misplaced. I wish I had seen that then. We needed that argument, but not to yell at each other.

"None of this is my choice!" I protested, my heart aching from the weight.

"Is that it? You want more? A choice? Well, what if you get to choose? What if you did and you chose wrong?"

"What are you talking about?"

"That day on the ship—"

"You know I have no memory of—"

"That day my mother asked me if I wanted to go with her to Tabashi," she said, the whole truth rendering me speechless. "I could have gone with her on the ship. I could have been there."

"Rimi—"

"I had the choice," she said—and then she cried, breaking in front of me. Her tears fell harder than any storm I could command. "I had a choice . . . and now I live with what I chose."

"Rimi," I said again, with all the tenderness that had been missing from our fight. I stepped towards her, but she pulled away from me so quickly that she took all the air left in the hall. "I'm so sorry," I tried again, but she was already gone, disappearing down the corridor with the shadows that creep in to tell you it's too late to fall asleep. I stared into the emptiness she left and saw the face of Alewic reaching for a daughter he could not comfort; because how do you offer someone their own forgiveness?

"Give her time," I heard quietly from behind a pillar. I turned to see Linh come out from the shadows. "She wouldn't yell at you if she didn't think it was worth it."

"How much did you hear?" I asked. I was shaking.

"Enough," she said tenderly. She came closer and into the light of the halls. "I remember you and Mira used to fight like that."

Mira.

Reader, that's her name. My best friend. The last chip. So there it is, and there I am without it—crumbling. Her name broke open the dam that was already barely holding on, giving way to the force of rain that had been collecting for decades.

"You don't have time," Linh said to me in my downpour, her voice urgent with fear. She opened my hands and placed into them a small sheathed dagger with a sapphire pressed into the hilt, the one I had hidden beneath the mattress—but how had she known? Before I could even ask, Linh pointed behind her to a dimly lit hall through the open archway.

"Turn right at the statue, then follow the stone path and pass through the gates. Head for the Jungle."

"Are you mad?" I scoffed, but I fastened the dagger around my waist as Linh helped me out of the metal framework that was still clinging to my body, holding me back. I knew she was right.

"You had always planned to run away together," she said. Her face was so serious. "I would be wrong to send you in there had I not seen you tonight. You'll be okay. I know it."

"And you?" I asked.

"I don't exist," she said with a soft smile. In her, I saw the reflection of a girl I once was, sheltered in the calm before the storm. A girl who sought solace in her silence, ceaselessly drifting from one life to the next, never questioning, and thus never choosing. I wondered whether this was her first decision, or simply the next in a series of countless remarkable ones yet to come.

"Thank you," I murmured through the hot tears streaming down my burning cheeks. Then I left without another word—my feet carrying me swiftly, as though they knew precisely where to guide me.

* * *

My heart pounded in my chest as I raced through the shadows, the cries of the guards growing fainter with each passing tide. I refused to be part of the Council's plans, tossed around like grain and at the mercy of the current. I shook their hands from my body. What could I do to make sure that my powers would not be a curse?

To forge a better path—I had to—and one that I got to choose. Stories be damned, the tapestries of old. Titles meant nothing if you hadn't earned the power of them. This time was ours and we had to make do with it what we could, both for ourselves and for those who believed in us, if they still did, if they could ever forgive me; that too I would have to earn.

Know who you are, and decide what you do.

I had so many questions, but the answers lay in the places they taught me to fear, the place I ran towards. No more hallowed halls and rooms covered in murals with stories I had no part in, windows to stare longingly out of. I wanted answers, and it was time I demanded them. Beside me, racing through the night, the faintest glow of the moonlight dancing on the dew that collected on the leaves—a watery wisp of smoke that followed me along my path, tethered to a name and a memory I held like a lifeline.

Lahela Tabashi.

I am Lahela Tabashi.

I look out to the sea in the face of a growing storm, and I welcome the rain.

Acknowledgments

I would like to thank my publisher for believing in this story, my editor for working with me through all of my first-author syndrome, my best friend for listening to my many hours of panicked voice notes, my *boarding house* sisters for seeing me through the many versions of myself it took to get here, my family for everything they've sacrificed and held on to, my mentors for being a beacon in the dark, *and bunny; thanks for bringing me out m'shell.* To everyone else that has graced my life to make me the person I am today; thank you—thank you.

To you, Reader. This book carries within it my whole heart—and then some. I wouldn't trade it for the world. A little girl who loved her stories held her first finished manuscript and smiled; thank you for reading it.

About the Author

MICHELE GOULD is a multidisciplinary artist, and her debut play was about dungeons and dragons. With a biomedical degree that she doesn't use, and a busy brain full of wacky ideas, she is deeply committed to writing diverse stories about underrepresented heroes. A big believer in radical self love and basking in the sunshine, you can find her @itsmichelegould trying to be the change she wants to see in the world.

Publisher's Note

A special thank you to the individuals who backed this production without knowing what they would receive. Your trust means everything and I hope you enjoyed the journey. Thank you.

Manufactured by Amazon.com.au
Sydney, New South Wales, Australia